RAVE REVIEWS FOR THE WORK OF

SHANNON DRAKE

Also available from *New York Times*
bestselling author

and HQN Books

The Queen's Lady
Beguiled
Reckless
Wicked

Watch for her next sweeping tale in fall 2009

SHANNON DRAKE

THE PIRATE BRIDE

HQN™

ISBN-13: 978-0-373-77316-9
ISBN-10:   0-373-77316-1

THE PIRATE BRIDE

For Bobbi Smith—
wonderful writer,
amazing friend.

THE PIRATE BRIDE

PROLOGUE

Victory and Defeat
The West Coast of Scotland
1689

"THE CHILD! For the love of God, Fiona, you must save the child."

The wind was stark and cold. Fiona's vision blurred, and she could do nothing but feel, and what she felt was a cold wind blowing. All her life, she had loved her home. The rich colors of the braes, the hard rock of the cliffs and crags, and aye, even the wicked cold and bitter wind that came with winter. Despite the chill, a day such as today often meant the coming of the spring, when the earth would burst forth with a wild beauty that was beloved by those who knew it and held in awe by those who did not. Aye, good God, but she loved her home, all the brilliant blues and mauves of spring, and the rich greens of summer…even the gray of an angry and overcast winter's day.

All swept away now.

By the bloodred spill of life that had been the final result of William III's so called "glorious revolution."

"Fiona!" She felt her husband's hands on her shoulders, shaking her. She opened her eyes and stared into his, and she knew then that she would never see him again. They were to pay. The Highland Scots were to pay for their opposition to William, for their loyalty to the legal king, James II. Catholic or no, by God's right, he should be king. And the Highlanders had proven their mettle—as they had so many times before—but it had been in vain, and now they were to be thrashed ruthlessly and without mercy in return.

"Ye've got to go now, my love. I'll be with you soon enough, I'll warrant," Mal told her, his eyes shifting from hers as he smoothed a stray lock of hair from her forehead.

"Ye'll not see me again," she whispered. At first she didn't feel the pain of that realization, only the whipping of the wind. But then she saw the endless blue of his eyes, the rich waves of his nearly midnight hair and the rugged planes of his face. His mouth was broad, his lips generous. She thought of his smile, of his kiss.

And suddenly the pain was like a knife ripping through her. She cried out and fell to her knees, and he quickly knelt down beside her, ignoring the men who awaited him, both his cavalry and his foot soldiers. It was not so regimented an army as the one that came after them, or the one they had so recently and brilliantly beaten with skill and daring. They were Highlanders, clansmen, and aye, they could feud, but when they fought together, it was as brothers. Still, they had their own minds and did not always need orders. But they had their hearts and souls when their weapons were poor. They would die for one another, in a bond not often found in the paid ranks of the enemy's army.

"Fiona, come." He reached out to help her to her feet. She saw his hands as they took her own, and they were wonderful hands, strong, long-fingered, capable of holding her with passion and a child with tenderness. She was suddenly terrified that she would shame him by screaming hysterically at the knowledge that he was going to die. And his death would be a crime against God, against nature, for he was a beautiful man in his strength and wisdom, not only in his flesh, and in the love he felt for the land and their God and all those who lived in their small corner of the world.

"The child, Fiona. You must protect the child."

She staggered to her feet, trying to see despite the curtain of her tears. She stood tall and reached a hand to the child standing near, wide-eyed, afraid, and yet so sadly old before time could make the years go by.

Mal suddenly bowed his head, perhaps to fight the dead light of destiny in his own eyes, then clasped his offspring, shaking.

Then he straightened and planted a last, fiercely sweet kiss upon her lips. "Gordon, take my lady and my child, and see them safe."

Malcolm turned then, taking his horse from one of his men, a distant cousin, as were so many. Gordon's hand fell upon her shoulders. "To the tender, my lady, swiftly now."

She was blinded. It was the wind, she told herself, but she knew it was the tears that streamed down her face, unheeded. As they raced to the shore, she wiped her cheeks and turned, lifting her babe, looking back one last time on the man she so loved.

Laird Malcolm, kilted and magnificent, sat upon his great charger, shouting to the men around him. And from the shore she could see the valiant charge of the Scots as they raced up the hill, their battle cry upon their lips.

They would die well.

They would not be dragged to the gallows and mocked as they died. Warriors all, they would battle their enemies to the death. Mal had claimed they would triumph, as they had done before, but she knew of a certainty that this time courage would not be enough.

In her arms, her young one squirmed. Ah, but so strong and tall already! "Me da!"

"Aye, Father goes to battle," she murmured.

Then, high atop the hill, she saw the enemy.

They came in one great mass. Thousands…and thousands…

She turned, tall, straight, no tears flowing down her cheeks now. With Gordon helping her along, she hurried to the water, where the tender waited. An oarsman, cloaked, his head down, sat ready.

"Hurry, man, hurry!" Gordon cried. "Ye must get her to the ship."

The oarsman rose and cast back his hood, and she looked in the man's eyes. Her heart leapt to her throat as she saw his face.

"Nay, I shall not," the oarsman said.

Gordon drew his sword, but the oarsman was ready. As fine and experienced a warrior as Gordon, his hand was already at the hilt of his sword beneath his cloak, and when he lifted his blade, it was to slice Gordon through.

She no longer felt or heard the wind. Her vision was clear now, and all she saw was red. A sea of it before her...

Madness struck her then. She reached for the dirk in the sheath at her waist, and she attacked.

The oarsman screamed in pain and rage, and responded instantly.

Fiona never felt the steel as it ripped into her. She heard her heart, though. Thumping, erratic and fast, pumping out her life's blood....

Her heart cried out. *Malcolm, my love, it seems that in truth we do not part after all today, for there is a heaven for those who have been just and strong....*

"Mother!"

Her child! Her precious child! She tried to cry out, but she had no breath.

As she lay dying, she heard his laughter.

And then there was screaming. But the sound did not come from her. As the world faded, she was dimly aware that the oarsman was pushing off from shore, and her child, still so young, yet old enough to see, to know what was happening, was being swept away by sheer evil.

CHAPTER ONE

The Caribbean
Pirates' Alley
1716

"Outgunned, outsailed, outmanned, out...blasted! Damn it all! Bring her about and set to speed. Full sail," Logan Haggerty cried, teeth grating, eyes narrowed, fury all but blinding him as he stared at the pirate ship headed his way.

"Captain, we *are* at full sail, and blimey, we're tryin' to come about," Logan's first mate, Jamie McDougall assured him. Jamie was an old salt, an honest merchantman impressed into the navy, he'd moved on to piracy and then been pardoned back into the King's own service. If there were a trick to be played upon the brine, Jamie knew it.

If there were a way to outrun a pirate, Jamie knew that, too.

If they were sunk through the greed and egotism of the aristocracy, well, Jamie would know that, as well.

Logan had informed the duke that there were pirates in the area and explained his own disadvantage due to the lack of manpower he had aboard, should they be boarded. He had explained, as well, that the weight of their cargo would drastically affect their speed and maneuverability.

But the duke hadn't cared.

Logan had ten guns.

The pirate had twenty he could easily count, perhaps more, and Logan's spyglass assured him that the crew upon the pirate vessel numbered at least two dozen men.

He traveled with a crew of twelve.

The vessel bearing down on them, sporting a scarlet flag, was handsome indeed. She was a sloop, sleek and fast, riding across the waves as smoothly as if she were soaring through the air. She had a narrow draft, and would easily be able to escape larger ships in the shallows. The craft was well-fitted, he could see. Besides the larger cannon pointing their way, he could see that the upper deck was fitted with a row of swivel guns, and those with many barrels.

She was a beauty and had been altered for her life of crime. Three masts, when many sloops offered but the mainmast, and with sails that caught the slightest breeze. Her tenders were situated behind the swivel guns, allowing no space for weakness. She was small, sleek and strong.

He had known better than to enter pirate territory, but pride had been his downfall.

Ah, yes, his own pride, even more than that of the nobility he mocked, who had tempted him into daring this voyage despite his original vehement refusal to accept the assignment.

And how had the duke managed that? Logan mocked himself then. Why, because of Cassandra.

Sweet Cassandra. He had been sure he could win her love if he just had enough money. His bloodline was noble enough, but his circumstances were far too impoverished to secure her to him. But if he made a success of this mission, he could return triumphant and regain all that his family had lost. No, that had been *stolen* from them. If he could challenge the sea and make this voyage, he would be worthy. *She* was the prize that mattered if he succeeded in this breakneck dash to bring the gold of the temple of Asiopia to the colonists in Virginia.

Now he realized that he had been a fool indeed. And why? What was it about the woman that had so beguiled him that he would attempt such a reckless endeavor? He had spent his life knowing he must make his own way, and he had known both harlots and great ladies. He had shown them courtesy one and all, but never had he felt such a tug upon his feelings, or this desire to settle down. It wasn't that she was a tease or temptress, that she made demands or ever threatened to play false. It was the laughter in her flashing, quicksilver eyes, the gentle touch of her fingertips, and, most of all, the honesty in her every word and action. He could love her; really love her. There was more, as well, of course, which he could admit in his own heart. She would be the perfect mate for him. She was the only child of a respected and wealthy family. With her name joined to his, he could reclaim all that had once been his family's, rebuild the Haggerty fortune. She was everything he could have hoped for in his life's partner.

He could not blame her for his own willingness to take this risk. He did not even blame her father, who merely wanted security for his only child.

If there was any blame, it fell only upon his own shoulders.

A mocking inner voice taunted him for a liar and a fraud.

He had said that he sailed because he needed the money, but that wasn't wholly true. He was always eager to sail the seas. Eager to find one man.

And that man lived upon the seas, outside the law.

Logan even claimed that he sought justice, not revenge, though were he honest with himself, he would have to concede that vengeance, too, was in his mind and heart.

He should have carried more guns, he told himself now. He should have brought more men, but he needed men he trusted for the battle he hoped to engage, and such men were hard to find.

Still, if there was any blame for his current predicament, it was his.

These were dangerous times to sail the seas. When England and Holland had been at war with Spain and France, many so-called pirates saw themselves as fighting a righteous battle. In an English ship, he would have been at the mercy only of a French or Spanish ship. But when the combatants had come to terms in 1697, privateers littered the sea.

Many had nothing to go home to.

Many had no desire to go home. Waging war upon the sea had become a way of life.

And many others saw that a fortune might be won if a man were brave, reckless and ready to risk his life.

Never before had the Caribbean been so overrun with thieves.

He rued fate and the wretched, greedy men who had lured him to go against his better judgment.

Damn them, he thought.

No.

Damn himself.

A man could not be led to such a place unless he chose his course.

So much for common sense and strength of purpose. He had fallen. And his own reckless desires had damned these good men along with him.

Here on the waves of the Caribbean, he would be the death of them all. They couldn't outrun the pirate ship, and they sure as hell weren't going to bring it down. He wasn't a coward, but neither was he a fool. Lust and greed were about to kill him and, worse, all these good men.

"M'lord Captain?" Jamie asked. "What is your command?"

"We must rely upon this pirate's honor," Logan said, knowing he must sacrifice pride for the sake of his men's lives.

"What?" Jamie demanded. "Pirates have no honor."

"Aye, they do. More than many a supposed great man," Logan said. "Send up the flag. Demand parley. I will negotiate with her captain."

"Negotiate?" Jamie protested. "There can be no negotiation—"

"If not, we are dead men. Bring our flag to half-mast. I will deal our way out of this," Logan said.

"Deal with a pirate captain? He'll skewer you through."

"Not if he wishes to keep the respect of his men," Logan assured him. "For the love of God, man, we are running out of time. Do as I say."

Despite Jamie's protest and the wary looks upon the faces of his men, in twenty minutes time they were broadside the pirate and not a cannon had been fired. Logan stood with his men, staring across at the handsome rigging of the pirate ship, while the crew of privateers stared at them, grinning, totally aware that they had the upper hand.

Grappling hooks and strong rope bound them as tightly together as lovers locked in an intimate embrace.

"Your captain, my fine fellows!" Logan shouted. "Where is your captain? I demand to see your captain."

"You *demand?*" one peg-legged man jeered.

"Indeed. It is my right to demand negotiation, not *even* though you be pirates but *because* you be pirates. If you refuse me, you are cursed and damned, and well you know it."

He had counted on the superstitious bent of sailing men, and he had not been mistaken. The surly crew muttered softly and looked uncertainly from one to another.

Then, through the crowd upon the deck, strode the

captain, a slender young man, clean-shaven, with rich dark hair curled beneath a broad-brimmed feathered hat. His coat was red velvet, and beneath it, his shirt was white as snow. He was tall with features that belonged on a Greek statue rather than a rogue at sea. He wore great black cuffed boots, and despite the elegance of his countenance, he walked with assurance, and the pistols and knife sheathed at his broad belt meant business, as did the long sword that hung by his side.

"Good heavens, men, don't let this gentleman disarm you so quickly. He is cleverly attempting to save his own hide," the pirate captain chided, stepping forward. "But not *even* because it is his supposed right to negotiate, but *because* he deems himself so clever, I am willing to take the time to have a word with the man."

"Whatever your reason, I appreciate it, good Captain…?" Logan said, waiting for a name.

"My flag tells it all," the captain said. "I'm known as Red Robert."

"You are an Englishman," Logan said, as if to remind the pirate he had attacked one of his countrymen. Though the days of so-called privateering were behind them, many a sea robber still did not prey upon his own kind.

"I am not an Englishman, I assure you."

Red Robert had apparently made his assessment already.

His name, Logan reflected, was bandied about in many a tavern. It was one that caused even the brave to tremble, for the stories that went about were fearsome.

He had not expected a man who looked so young. Then again, pirates rarely survived many years, at least, not at piracy. They were killed, or they took what riches they had obtained, changed their names and created new lives on distant islands or in out-of-the-way towns.

Logan spoke again, aware that he had to do so with a certain eloquence if he intended to achieve his goal of keeping his men alive, whatever his own fate.

He took a step forward. "I, good Captain Robert, am Logan Haggerty, Lord of Loch Emery, with no emphasis on the title, for were it worthy of great land or riches, you'd not be finding me here upon the high seas. What I seek is the right of man-to-man combat."

"Hmm, do tell," Red Robert said.

"If you best me with your sword, you have gained a good ship and great riches without spilling an ounce of blood other than my own, or chancing the loss of treasure to the bottom of the sea, and without risking the lives and limbs of your men."

"And if *you* best *me,* m'lord?" Red Robert inquired with polite amusement.

"Then we sail away."

Red Robert seemed to weigh his words with gravity. But then he said, "Surely you are jesting."

"Are you afraid?" Logan demanded, assessing the pirate captain's slender frame and apparent youth, which made a strange contrast indeed against the hardened edge of the sea robbers surrounding him.

"This is not a profession for one who is afraid," Red Robert returned casually. "Don't be deceived by my youth, *Lord* Haggerty. I am more than proficient with my weapons."

One well-muscled man standing at the pirate captain's side—not much older, but far stronger and broader—whispered in Red Robert's ear, causing him to laugh.

"This may be some trick, Red," one of the other men warned, a fellow with long gray hair, a large gold earring and his fingers twitching on the hilt of the knife at his waist.

"No trick," Logan said quietly.

"No fear, Hagar," Red said, acknowledging the man who had spoken. "And no deal." He turned to Logan. "However, here is what I do offer. If you best me, you do not sail away free. After all, m'lord, you surely knew you traveled dangerous waters." When Logan would have spoken, Red Robert raised his hand. "Your men live. They may sail away free with half the treasure. But you remain with us, a willing prisoner, to be held for ransom."

"I've told you. My title means little."

"And so the daring voyage you attempted today?" Red Robert mocked.

Logan stood his ground without reply, though his heart seemed to shrivel at the thought of never seeing Cassandra again. Still, his men would live to sail away.

If he could win.

And, God help him, the fellow was lean, which would make him quick. Agile. A deadly foe.

Though far broader in the shoulder himself, and not without a fair share of power in his arms, he was agile, as well. He'd trained with some of the finest swordsmen money could buy, since it was only recently that the family fortunes had taken such a sad turn.

His men. He had to save his men, God help him. He'd had every right to gamble with his own life, but he had been wrong to risk theirs, as well. And if he could best this captain...

"I will be your willing prisoner. But I would ask, then, that even if I lose, you take the treasure but give my men the tenders so that they might make safe landfall."

Red Robert shrugged.

The tall, dark-haired fellow at his side protested. "No."

The captain turned on him with such a fierce look of displeasure that the man stepped back and hung his head. "Brendan," Red said warningly.

The captain had a curious voice, Logan thought. He seemed eternally soft-spoken. Strange, for someone who needed to bellow orders against the wind. There was a husky, almost whispered quality to his voice.

"Aye, Red," the man named Brendan replied, but despite his immediate acknowledgment that Red was captain and his orders stood, he was rigidly disapproving.

"It is done," Red Robert said.

"This is madness," Jamie protested softly to Logan. "A trick, certainly. They will not let us go. They will not forego half of such a treasure."

"It *is* madness," Logan agreed. Madness from the moment he had agreed to transport the treasure. Madness? Aye, from start to finish, but here was his chance to at least save those he had dragged into folly along with him.

"Madness, but I believe this pirate will stand by his word."

"My deck, m'lord Captain, is the larger," Red Robert said. "We shall hold our contest here."

There was some muttering upon the pirate's deck.

And some protests from Logan's own.

Red Robert lifted a hand. The muttering went silent. "We shall fight until first blood," he called out gruffly.

"Are you afraid of Lord Haggerty's prowess?" Jamie shouted out.

Logan wished the man silent. They were hardly in a position to aggravate their opponents.

"I don't intend to sacrifice a fine ransom or ready muscles for the oars," Red returned, unruffled.

"Well?" demanded one of Red's fellows. "Do we get on with this or not?"

Logan leapt nimbly upon the ship's rail to make his way to the other ship's deck. Alone among the ruffians and sea robbers, he stood his ground. He stared at the slender and oddly aesthetic pirate, then dipped a deep and sweeping bow. "At your convenience, Captain."

"Clear the deck," Red Robert said, and it wasn't a resounding, thunderous shout, but a quiet command, still instantly obeyed.

"He needs a second!" Jamie McDougall called, and leapt across to stand, white-faced, fists clenched, at Logan's side.

Jamie McDougall was a good and loyal friend,

Logan thought. They had a long history together. Jamie would not, apparently *could* not, leave him now.

Red Robert pulled his sword from the handsome scabbard belted about his hip. He swept a courtly bow to Logan. "At your convenience, m'lord."

"Nay, sir, at yours," Logan said softly.

It might have been a casual meeting on the street. At first they circled one another carefully, each trying to assess the measure and mettle of the other man. Neither of them appeared the least concerned. Logan saw a smile twitch at the pirate's lips. This close, he saw that the captain was indeed very young.

He wondered that the pirate captain, however youthful and—perhaps?—inexperienced he might be, had not shed the crimson coat. He was clad in shirt and breeches himself, allowing a far greater freedom of movement.

But his opponent seemed perfectly comfortable in his coat.

He certainly wasn't about to suggest his opponent remove it. Why offer his foe any advantage?

"Get 'im, Red!" cried gray-haired Hagar, and a chant went up among the pirates.

Not to be outdone, Logan's own crew called encouragement to him.

"Take the sea robber, m'lord! Take him!" Jamie shouted.

"Red, watch his footwork," warned the man named Brendan.

"He's a scurvy sea rat, m'lord!" cried someone from his own deck. Richard Darnley, Logan thought, a good young sailor, and a man intent on making his way in the world.

Young and stalwart. A man who deserved a long life and the fulfillment of his dreams.

Red Robert continued to assess him.

And then they met.

Slowly, almost politely. A touching of the swords. A meeting of the eyes.

Then they began in earnest.

Logan felt the clash of steel vibrate all along his arm. A quick return, another, then another.

For a moment he felt he had the advantage, but he quickly realized he had thought too soon.

His opponent leapt nimbly against the starboard hull, then pushed off and nearly caught him dead in the chest. Logan managed a jump to the side, instinct-driven, and he was certain that saved his life. But it had been close. Far too close. They were fighting only until first blood was drawn. But had the pirate made good on that last lunge…

It wasn't to be a gentlemanly duel, Logan realized.

"M'lord, watch the wretched sea robber," Jamie warned him.

Logan came on hard with a series of quick thrusts and slashes, forcing his opponent back again. Just when he thought he had the pirate nearly cornered against the master's cabin, Red Robert once again made a sudden sweeping leap that sent him bouncing off a storage bin. This time when he came about, it was to nearly sever Logan's head from his body.

Instinct had driven him to duck, keeping life and

skull intact. Barely. His opponent was as adept with a sword as he'd claimed, and clearly not at all afraid of shedding blood or lopping off limbs.

Logan caught a glimpse of the pirate's eyes.

They were narrowed and deadly.

The chanting, the jests, the encouragement, the hoots of derision, all seemed to be getting louder and louder, like a growing storm.

The pirate's face was flushed. Red Robert wore his name well at that moment, Logan reflected, hoping he was seeing a sign of weakness. Perhaps the pirate had been a bit too impressed with his own skill. A more than respectable skill, certainly, but no man was assured of victory.

He had to take the advantage now, Logan knew. A very large part of excellence in swordsmanship lay in the mind, in creating a strategy for using a man's talents most effectively. A heavy man used his weight and strength, a nimble man his agility. To best this pirate, he had to assess each leap and slide the man might take beforehand, then be somewhere else when the strike came.

Once again the pirate took to the air, this time landing atop a rum barrel. And in that split second, Logan anticipated the man's next move, a rapid leap that would bring the pirate behind him.

Logan whirled around. In that brief moment, he prayed he hadn't anticipated in error and that the pirate would not come down behind his current position.

He didn't.

Too late, Red Robert saw that his move had been predicted.

He landed facing Logan.

And Logan set the point of his blade against the pirate's throat.

Blue eyes gazed at him with fury, and yet he was certain the pirate was not so much angry with him as he was with himself for being outmaneuvered.

"Good calculation," Robert said, barely managing to unclench his teeth.

Logan withdrew the point of his sword and bowed.

As he stood, he found the pirate's blade at his throat. It was his turn for anger.

"You, Captain, are not a man of your word. I have bested you."

The pirate gloated. "First blood. You did not draw blood."

"Only because I chose not to cause injury. But an agreement has been made, and I am an honest man."

"But I am a pirate."

"A pirate's honor is said to be greater than the average man's."

"And what do you know of a pirate's honor?" Red Robert demanded.

"I have sailed these seas for many years."

Red Robert's sword began to drop.

Still angry, Logan reacted, slashing hard against his opponent's blade and all but sending it flying. He quickly nicked the fellow's cheek; a tiny dot of blood appeared.

"First blood," he said icily.

Red Robert didn't even blink. Nor did he touch the drop of blood upon his cheek.

He merely turned away, striding toward the door to the master's cabin, where he paused, looking back and speaking to his men. "The cargo of our Lord Captain's ship shall be evenly divided. His men may proceed upon their path when our split of the goods has been taken."

"What of the captain himself?" Brendan asked.

"Take him below to the brig, of course," Red Robert said. Those icy blue eyes met Logan's across the deck. "He is an honorable man. He will go without skirmish, as he has sworn, I am certain."

"And if I were not a gentleman? If I were to protest now?" Logan inquired.

"You drew first blood, but I'm quite certain you realize I do not exaggerate my ability at swordsmanship," Red Robert said tightly. "I am equally adept with a cat-o'-nine-tails. But that's really no matter, is it? You gave your word. And you are a man of honor."

The pirate captain turned to enter the cabin.

"Wait!" Logan demanded.

Red Robert turned back.

"I would request a moment with my first mate. To give instructions."

"As you wish."

"You're not afraid it's a trick?" he could not help but ask.

"Why would I be afraid? I repeat, you have assured me that you are a man of your word."

Red Robert stepped through the cabin door.

Logan stood tall and straight, watching the door close. He felt as if he were trembling inside, but he could not—would not—let it show. He had achieved his aim; his men would live. They would sail on to South Carolina.

"My lad, my fine lord," Jamie said, and it sounded as if he were choking. He did not stand on ceremony. He gripped Logan's shoulders tightly, staring into his eyes with misery.

"Jamie, my good fellow. I'm quite all right. You will sail on with the others and see to my release. I believe our patrons will be glad half their treasure has survived, and you must ensure that we receive the promised cut. Forty percent. Don't take less."

"Aye, captain."

Logan saw that Brendan was leading a ten-man crew across to his ship.

Even from this distance, he could tell that his own men were tight-lipped and stiff, barely moving.

"Help with the divide," he called out, his voice strong. "We have made a deal, and it will be kept. Hinder no man of the pirate ship in his effort to take what is his."

"Ye heard the captain!" Jamie roared.

"Go, my friend. See to it," Logan told him.

Jamie nodded, deep sorrow in his eyes. The old salt actually looked as if he were about to cry.

"I have survived thus far," Logan assured him softly. He forced a cocky smile. "I guarantee you, I shall continue to do so."

"I will find a way to kill these blasted brigands," Jamie swore. "I'll not rest 'til I've met whatever ransom this pirate requires and seen you freed."

"You are a good man, Jamie. We will meet again."

"M'lord…"

"Tell Cassandra…" Logan began.

"Aye?"

"Tell her that I am deeply sorry. But that…that I pray—no, I demand!—that she choose whatever path now lies open to her for happiness."

"Nay, my lord!"

"You will tell her so, Jamie. Swear it to me."

"I cannot—"

"You can. You must. Swear it, Jamie."

Jamie hung his head. "Aye, Logan. As you wish."

"Go with God, Jamie."

Jamie, a fierce and bitter look upon his face, glanced toward the captain's cabin.

"I pray that God will be with you, for surely he has abandoned all other men here."

"He helps those who help themselves, so it is said, and I am quite capable of helping myself, as you know, my friend."

Jamie nodded tightly, then turned quickly and moved on.

Logan remained.

Feeling the breeze.

The sea…the air…the sweet cry of the wind. They all meant freedom to him. He had never realized just how much until this moment. Amazing how he had never before realized how much he had loved freedom.

But then…

It was a long time since he had been a prisoner.

That had been another lifetime. But he hadn't forgotten.

After all, that memory was half the reason for the fool trip that had brought him to this fate.

"M'lord Captain?"

There was just a hint of mockery in the words.

Brendan stood at his side, watching him. The fellow neither smiled nor goaded him as he continued. "I'm afraid your presence is required. In the brig."

Logan nodded.

The man carried shackles, he noticed.

"There is no need for those," he said. "Merely show me the way."

The man did so, first looking toward his captain's cabin, then sweeping an arm toward the steps that led down to the hold.

With one last glance at the brilliant blue sky, Logan headed for the steps.

They seemed to lead to blackness, to an abyss.

But one no darker than his heart.

To take risks was one thing.

To lose all…

Quite another.

His men had lived. And he thanked God that in all his years, even through his bouts of rage-inspired madness, he had never forced others to perish on any quest of his making.

He had never meant to sell his soul.

But as he descended into the darkness, he wondered if he had lost it anyway.

CHAPTER TWO

THE SOUND WAS haunting, would always be haunting...

There were hoofbeats coming like thunder. A slow rumble at first, like a tremor pulsing beneath the earth. With the first vibration, it seemed as if the birds screamed, followed by the rushing of the wind. The sound of the hoofbeats grew louder, the quivering of the earth, deeper. Then, a mere heartbeat later, the pounding hooves came ripping through grass and dirt, striking sparks off rock, shaking the world.

By the time the horses raced into view, there was screaming everywhere. People were running, desperate.

The thunder was upon them. As loud as if a bolt of lightning had struck the ground and blasted a hole through the globe.

Then...

A sword, glittering in the sun.

The blood, a cascade of it, gushing, flying...turning the blue day to red.

And the bodies...

Red awoke gasping, stunned and frightened, but aware that someone was there, someone with strong hands, and a frantic and yet somehow reassuring whisper.

"Stop. Don't scream."

Red let out a shaky sigh, gulping for air, but remained silent.

"You haven't had the nightmare in a long time."

Red nodded.

"It was the fight," Brendan said.

"I don't know what it was," Red said curtly.

"I do," Brendan said. "It was the duel."

Red was silent.

"Do you think he knows?" Brendan asked anxiously.

Red straightened and rose, escaping Brendan's touch, to pace the confines of the master's cabin.

"I don't know."

"You scared me to death, you know," Brendan said, getting to his feet, as well. He caught Red by the shoulders and looked into those striking blue eyes. "You could have been killed."

"I could have been killed a dozen times over the past few years," Red said.

That was true enough.

Brendan released Red and began pacing himself. "The fellow is clever, too clever. I mean, what fool transporting such treasure would dare such a brazen ploy? God knows, most pirates would not have bowed to such a bargain."

Red sank down on the elaborate sofa that flanked the handsome mahogany desk. "No?" The reply was dry. "I seem to recall successfully using a similar ploy against the great Blackbeard himself."

Brendan paused and stared at Red. "Blackbeard told me he was amazed when he met you, fascinated, and that he thought you such a *pretty* boy it amused him not to kill you. He seemed quite baffled by his own response."

"I beat even the great Edward Teach fairly," Red told him indignantly.

Brendan shook his head. "Only because at first he was laughing so hard that he underestimated you. He knew you were a woman, Bobbie. He admired you tremendously."

"A good thing, since he is still a friend and has kept my secret," she said sharply. "And that is the thing, Brendan. Most the fellows we run into are vermin-ridden and desperate men, keen on making their fortunes—yet easily swayed by a bottle of rum and a whore. But even those filthy, rotten-toothed knaves usually have a certain honor. Honor among thieves, if you will. But they have shown more honor than most of the supposedly respectable noblemen with whom we've come in contact. They adhere to the pirate's code of ethics. We did nothing less today."

"I fear he knows," Brendan said darkly.

"So what? Our whole crew knows," she pointed out.

"The whole crew worships you. You saved them from certain death," he reminded her. "An act you might have found yourself hanged for, by *law*."

She shrugged. At the time, there had been nothing else to do. That had been her first act as a pirate. She had done exceptionally well, taking everything into consideration. "We might have died, as well. There was no guarantee for the future when we began. We were already impersonating others, even then."

A quick smile curled Brendan's lips. "You did go from being Lady Cuthbert to Red Robert with amazing speed. You could have done remarkably well on the stage."

Red had been smiling, as well, but now her smile faded. "Aye, and what good would a life on the stage do me? I'd be considered no more than a harlot at that, either."

"You would live to a grand old age, perhaps," Brendan said.

"That wouldn't be living. Brendan, I cannot forget…"

"That's evident. Your screams are terrible. I thank God I was able to transform that closet around the corner into a first-mate's chamber. If you scream so and I cannot stop you before you are heard, we will be in serious trouble."

"The nightmare hasn't come in almost a year," she said.

Brendan went to his knees at her feet, touching her cheek tenderly. "We are living a dangerous lie. A very dangerous lie."

She touched his face in return. "I'm all right. I swear it. I will not dream again."

"You can't know that! We need to—"

"Turn back?"

"Aye, Bobbie, we must turn back."

Roberta stood again. "I will never turn back."

"But, Bobbie…"

She stared at him, minus the dark wig, minus the boots and knives and pistols, the coat and the plumed hat. Her real hair was red, and it streamed down her back in soft glistening curls in the glow of the lamplight. She knew that, minus her trappings, she appeared almost frail and ethereal. She knew and loved her own crew, especially Hagar, who had been their friend before. They would never harm her, and they would die before they saw her harmed. But her facade was a strong one, because it was necessary. And no matter how she appeared in the dead of night, in truth, the ruthlessness she showed in pursuit of her cause, the strength and determination, were now the reality of who she was.

"There are no buts, Brendan. Now, beloved cousin, we both need to get some sleep."

"I still fear he knows," Brendan said dourly.

She smiled at him sweetly. "Then he'll have to die."

"I STILL SAY YOU take too many risks."

Logan was startled, in his prison below the deck, by the words he heard so clearly. He'd spent the last two days in a small hold, walled away from the cargo. At some point it might have been private quarters for a ship's officer, but now it was barren of anything—anything at all. It was a ten-by-ten wooden space, but there were two small horizontal windows, perhaps ten inches long and three inches high, and he had listened at them constantly, hearing whatever he could of the crew's conversations.

They hadn't said much. But after two days of solitude broken only by the arrival of a tray of food three times a day, along with fresh water and a small portion of rum, any conversation was, if not elucidating, at least momentarily entertaining.

He'd wondered frequently just how long his imprisonment would last. It was certainly not the worst punishment he might have received. No whips had been brought against his back, he hadn't been starved, or threatened with death or mutilation...but the monotony, after only two days, was numbing. He'd spent his first hours seeking a means of escape, then sought for one again, even when he realized there was but one door and it was kept closed by a massive lock. The crew were diligent and took no chances. Several armed men came to the door each time food was delivered.

He spent hours mock-dueling with himself with no sword, hours pacing the small confines, and hours thinking. The thinking he tried to stop. It led him nowhere.

This time, though, it was very late in the night, and the ship had been quiet for hours. And the voices he heard now belonged to Red Robert and his first mate, Brendan.

Red let out a soft chuckle. "Ah, but what is life *but* risk?"

"Yes, but up until now you've had a plan, and now...now you're risking your life."

"Brendan, stop this obsession. We risk our lives every morning when we awake and take a breath."

Brendan let out a sigh of aggravation.

"You shouldn't have kept the prisoner."

"I should have killed them all?"

"No." There was a silence. "Damned good ship, though, and you let it sail away."

"We don't need another ship."

"We didn't need a prisoner."

"What difference does his presence make? We may find someone willing to pay for his release."

"Right. He was out on the seas stealing from the ancients when we came upon him," Brendan said dryly.

"A man has to make his own fortune, but that doesn't mean there isn't someone out there willing to pay for his release."

Brendan grunted. "He'll go mad by the time you let him out."

"No harm has been done to him."

"Imprisonment can destroy the mind. You've left him with nothing. Not a book…not a thing. He can't even practice tying knots."

"Give a man a rope, he may hang himself," the captain pointed out.

"He's able-bodied."

"Too able-bodied," Red snapped.

"He could work."

"And he could escape. *Kill* someone and escape."

"He wouldn't," Brendan said.

I wouldn't?

"Oh?" Red asked.

"He's a man of his word."

"And he's given his word not to escape?"

"You haven't asked him for it."

"He isn't being tortured," Red said impatiently.

"He could be useful on deck."

"We don't need a deckhand."

Brendan sniffed. "We're not a large group, you know."

"Nor can we be."

"So we can use another deckhand."

Red groaned and fell silent.

"Look, when this began…I understood. But now…what exactly are you looking for?" Brendan's voice sounded both sad and serious.

There was silence, then a soft reply. "Revenge. It's what keeps me going. It's my only reason to stay alive."

He heard footsteps; then the captain called to one of the men, checking on the ship's heading. They were going in a southwesterly direction, and Logan couldn't help wondering why.

He leaned back against the wall thoughtfully. The captain was indeed young. But for one so young, there was something ageless in his outlook. Revenge, not life, was not the most worthy prize. How had one so young come to hate so much?

Maybe it wasn't all that difficult. Such was the wretchedness of life that many were born to endure. Some rose above it. Some barely survived it.

Some died.

And some became cutthroats, thieves and pirates.

But Red Robert…something about him was different. He was so small and almost…effete, extremely adept of course, but hardly…manly.

Logan leaned back in deeper thought, and in a few

minutes he knew he had to be right about the conclusion he had come to.

But…*why?*

And just what revenge could drive someone to such desperate measures?

Logan was cuffed when he was taken from his cubicle in the cargo hold. Brendan apologized, as two men took care of the actual shackling. "Sorry, my friend. But we respect your talents, and thus…well, I'm sure you understand."

Logan nodded gravely. "Thank you, *my friend.* I will take that as a compliment."

Brendan shrugged. He led the way past the first hold, with its guns, powder, crates of cargo and supplies, and crew hammocks, and then topside. Ah, topside. Fresh air. It was clean and clear, and the breeze was soft and beautiful. No rain was on the horizon, and no storm clouds threatened the heavens. He was glad for a minute just to stand there, to feel the embrace of the sun.

But then a hand was clamped on his shoulder, and he was led toward the aft cabin. Brendan knocked on the door and received a crisp "Aye" from Captain Robert.

Brendan nodded to Logan, indicating that he should enter. As the door closed behind him, Logan found the captain, fully dressed in breeches, shirt, vest, coat, boots and hat, seated at a large mahogany desk and writing with a quill pen. He did not look up at Logan's entry, nor when he spoke.

"It's been brought to my attention that although your

welfare certainly means little enough, you might be of use on deck, though I confess I do not trust you. That being said, my mate seems to believe you would be willing to give your oath that you would make no foolish attempts at escape, were we to set you to work topside." The quill was set into the inkpot. The captain looked up at last. "Quite frankly, if you did try to escape, we would have to kill you. Not a great loss to us, I'm afraid, but as you are certainly adept with weapons, I would be loathe to lose a loyal crew member over you. The choice is yours."

Crisp words, hard spoken, no humor on the face, the facade quite effective.

"I don't even know where we are. I'm not at all sure where I could escape *to*. The waters of the Caribbean are warm, but vast," he replied.

"That's not exactly an oath. Try to escape now, and yes, you would die, one way or the other. And, as I said, it means little to us, since there's no guarantee we can gain any reward whatsoever for your life." The pirate was staring at him intently. Those eyes were…

Deep blue. And haunting.

"I give you my word, Captain, that I will not try to escape while working topside," Logan said, his tone as level and emotionless as the captain's.

The captain assessed him with a direct and emotionless stare. And then…just the slightest hint of a smile. "Good. It's laundry day."

"Laundry?" Logan said incredulously.

"Aye, laundry."

"But…we're at sea."

"Aye, that we are."

"But you'd be wasting good water!"

"What I waste is my concern. There is a Bible on the edge of my desk. Place your hand upon it and swear you will not try to escape." Again, a subtle smile upon the captain's lips. The young face could be gamine-like, delicate…beautiful, beneath the attempt at ruggedness. "*And* that you will do laundry." Red picked up the quill again and began to write. "And bathe."

"Bathe?" Logan inquired politely.

"There's a breeze today, you may have noticed. Otherwise, the Caribbean is quite hot. What many of my associates upon these seas have not noticed is that we seem to avoid the dangers of disease with greater success than others because we make every attempt to keep this vessel free from vermin, such as rats, and the lice that are prone to so enjoy the human scalp and body. When we are at anchor, by the islands, my men are quite fond of swimming. They have discovered that saltwater is excellent for whatever may be plaguing their skin. So, you will serve—and bathe—as one of us. Or you may rot back in the cargo hold."

"Captain, bathing does not at all dissuade me."

"And laundry?"

"It will be a new…adventure," he admitted.

"Adventure," Red mused. "Well, then. Swear. On the Bible."

"Do most of your captives believe in God, Captain?"

"Most men claim not to give a damn if the devil takes them, but I don't believe you're the average man.

Then again, at the point of death, a man's beliefs have a tendency to change. I've seen many a supposed disbeliever cry out to heaven when he knows his death is imminent. So, swear or return to the brig."

He picked up the Bible and gave his oath.

When he set it down he said, "Laundry…and bathing. I can only assume then, given that I have correctly ascertained our direction, we're heading for Nassau."

"Nassau, New Providence. You know it?" Red asked politely. "You don't appear to be the type of man who spends much time there."

"I've been there," Logan said.

"Well?" Red demanded, when Logan continued to stand there.

"Will I be allowed to go ashore?"

"Yes."

"How magnanimous of you."

Red turned those striking eyes full on him. "Pirates do have honor, as you keep pointing out to me. I will see to it that everyone is made aware that you are a captive and where you belong. Should you attempt to escape, any one of them would happily kill you, because we'll have a bounty on your head, a fair sum for your return—dead or alive," Red said pleasantly.

"That won't be necessary," Logan said.

"Really?"

"I have given my word. And, Captain, if you're curious, I do believe in God, in the hereafter and in purgatory. I prefer to spend my full share of years upon this earth, but I am not afraid to die."

"Bravo," Red said dryly.

"*You* are obviously not afraid to die," Logan said.

Red once again set down the quill. "You said it so well, Lord Haggerty. I would prefer to spend my time upon the earth, rather than beneath it—or as fish food, as might well be my fate. But I am not afraid of death. You may go now."

"I am handcuffed."

"So you are."

"It's difficult to do laundry in handcuffs."

"That matter will be rectified."

"Captain Red Robert…" Logan said musingly.

"What now?"

"You, too, do not seem to be the type of…man to spend time in New Providence."

"And why is that?"

"I've not seen all that many well-bathed gentlemen upon the island."

"I have certainly never claimed to be a gentleman, much less do I claim the title of 'lord.'"

"I definitely do claim it—it just doesn't mean a great deal."

"Many a man buys his bath on New Providence," Red said impatiently.

"Yes, and many other things." Logan grinned knowingly, as one man to another.

"Are you talking just to annoy me, or to avoid doing laundry?"

Logan smiled. "Well, it *is* in the articles of piracy that there should be no women aboard a ship. Bad luck, you know and brawls between the men."

"If you're asking me if you can buy a whore on the island, Lord Haggerty, you might want to recall that you are a captive, and as such, you have no coin."

Logan was still grinning. "That would be 'no,' then?"

"Do you wish to return to the brig?" Red demanded.

"Not at all. I am quite intrigued by the concept of laundry."

"Aye, I don't imagine a lord knows much about it."

"I pronounce it 'laird,'" Logan said, surprised by his own sudden irritability.

"A Scotsman, then?" Red said politely. "I had noticed the accent."

"Indeed."

Red stared at him. "No better than an Englishman, I'm afraid." Red's voice rose. "Brendan!"

The door opened; Brendan was waiting.

Logan cleared his throat and lifted his hands. "You have my word," he said seriously.

"Captain, seeing as the man has sworn, may I remove the shackles?"

Red Robert had returned to the quill and paper but gave a slight nod.

Brendan grinned. Logan realized the captain's right-hand man liked him, or at least respected him. He realized, as well, that Brendan bore a resemblance to the captain, or vice versa. They were both far too young for this life.

Then again, few grew old in it.

"Laundry, I'm afraid," Brendan said.

Logan shrugged. "Lead me to it."

SHE HEARD LAUGHTER on deck.

Laughter!

Red stood and walked to the cabin windows. Shifting the drape slightly aside, she stared at the improbable sight on deck. The men were teaching their prisoner the art of laundry.

He had already found himself a comfortable niche within the group, which told her that he was either a fearless idiot or very brave indeed. Either way, he was dangerous.

There was a knock at the door, which opened before Red could find out who was there or ask him to enter. It was Brendan.

"Aha!" he said. "You're spying on our captive."

"I'm the captain," Red said irritably. "I can spy on anyone I want."

"The captain." Brendan laughed, then sat, placing his feet up on her desk, at ease and amused. "He's quite a man, is he not?"

"Interesting, at least."

"And a good swordsman."

"Yes, I noticed." A finger rose to her cheek, as if on its own.

"It's a nick. It won't scar."

"I am scarred to the quick as it is, Brendan."

"Ah, but that's your soul, not your flesh."

Red shooed him away from the desk and sat herself. "We're heading for New Providence."

"Aye, that's been your course. But—"

"We can sell this new cargo there."

"We can get more for it in the colonies."

"I don't want to travel so far with this much treasure. Word of what we have will get out, and we'll be under attack by every untrustworthy sailor out there. It may be considered ill luck to attack a fellow pirate, but most of the time our peers are greedier than they are superstitious."

Brendan was silent for a while before changing the subject. "I know I have been tormenting you lately, but you must know this life we lead can't go on forever. How long do you plan to carry on this charade?"

"As long as it takes."

He leaned forward. "It grows more dangerous every day. And I don't like going into Nassau. It's a lair of the worst filth known to humanity. The fellow sharing your rum bottle one moment will gladly share his dagger the next."

"That's why the entire crew is careful and ever watchful of one another's backs," Red said.

Brendan shook his head. "You want to go to Nassau to see if you can't find out where *he's* heading."

"Of course."

Brendan fell silent again.

"Will you please stop fretting?" Red finally demanded, aggravated.

"Lately…lately I've been afraid, I admit. Look, we've done well…we could find some place, assume new identities…we could live decent lives. Real lives. There are places in America where we could disappear."

"It isn't about money, Brendan."

Brendan shook his head. "Bobbie, you know the

kind of man he is. He's going to be killed by someone, somewhere."

"Oh, really? He's managed to spend nearly two decades making his fortune off the terror and tragedy of others. Besides, I would prefer to kill him myself," Red said sharply. "And stop calling me Bobbie, please. I'm Captain Red."

Brendan looked aggravated. "You're Roberta, Bobbie to me, no matter what charade we're playing. We've survived this far together, but we used to be…you used to listen to me. I have a terrible feeling we've taken things too far."

The set of Red's features was stubborn. "Brendan," she said, and there was steel in her voice, as well as a certain compassion, "if you wish to quit, you may do so. I can set you ashore at a safe harbor of your choosing, and you can take passage on a ship to the colonies. You can claim to have been the victim of a kidnapping for all the time we've been at sea, God knows, it will not have been the first such time that has happened."

"Bobbie, God knows I have fought, and fought hard, at your side. I have risked my life, just as you have risked yours."

"No one has fought harder," she agreed.

"But I can't help but admit to this strange desire to survive."

"I want to survive, too. Instinct, I suppose."

"There is a life out there for you…somewhere."

"Brendan, what, in all the time that we have shared together, have I known that might be construed as an actual *life?*"

She saw the pain in his eyes. Brendan had shared so much with her from the beginning. Terror. Poverty. Servitude, threats, abuse, and an elite governing body that had turned its collective back upon them. She had finally discovered the only true kinship she had ever known among the pirate brethren.

Brendan rose suddenly. "Who knows? Maybe if our wretched old mistress had sent you off to a decent and compassionate—albeit old and disease-riddled—man, things would have been different."

She cast him a furious stare.

"What a wonderful suggestion, Brendan. I could have lived a wretched life as a syphilitic whore and then died a wretched death. I'll take a sword," she added softly.

"Bobbie—"

"Stop calling me Bobbie!"

"The men know your name."

"Our prisoner does not."

"The prisoner you've been spying on. If you're so intrigued, come out and join your men, Captain Red Robert."

"If you wish to be nothing but a pest, you should leave and enjoy the company of the prisoner and the men," Red said irritably.

"I'll do so," Brendan said, and grinned.

When he was gone, Red stared at the door, wondering why she felt so ridiculously annoyed. And worried. Brendan's certainty that they had taken their act-turned-real-life too far was beginning to make her uneasy despite herself. She gritted her teeth, looking at the lists she was preparing regarding the division of their take. The words seemed to swim before her. She was getting cabin fever. She had stayed locked up in her small realm on the ship for too long. She needed air.

Brendan's accusations were true. She *was* obsessed. But *he* was out there. And she meant to find him, to kill him, or die in the trying.

Blair Colm.

So many years had passed. But if she closed her eyes…

When she slept too sweetly…

She could see it all again as if it had happened just yesterday. They'd been but children then.

There were men who fought because they fought for a cause. Others sought riches, titles, to better themselves in life.

And some were simply cruel. Some enjoyed watching the pain they caused others. They considered it only a bonus that slicing men, women and children to death often came with a reward, as well. Blair Colm was one of those men.

It was amazing that she and Brendan had survived….

But there had been so many others to kill.

And so they had been sold into indentured servitude in the colonies instead.

She had hated Lady Fotherington almost as much as she had hated Blair Colm. Prim, bony, iron-haired, iron-willed, she had thought that indentured servants did best when beaten at least once a week. To her way of thinking, certain nationalities created beings of lesser value, and Roberta and Brendan were certainly that.

Red looked at her hands, and sniffed. It had not been difficult to play the part of a man as far as the delicacy of her hands went. She had spent her days scrubbing…anything from the hearth in the kitchen to Ellen Fotherington's hideous feet. The only kindness she had ever known had come from Ellen's spinster daughter, Lygia. As tall and thin and bony as her mother, she rarely spoke in front of anyone. Red had finished with her tasks late one night and slipped into the office that had belonged to the late Lord Fotherington, and had found Lygia there, reading. Red had been terrified, certain she would receive an extra beating, but the great rows of books had beckoned to her forever. Stammering, she had tried to think up an excuse, but Lygia had actually smiled, and the smile had made her, if not beautiful, compelling. "Shh. I'm not supposed to be here, either. I am supposed to follow other arts, such as music and dance, but I do so love my father's room. If only he had lived…."

He hadn't lived, however. He had died of a flux. And so Ellen Fotherington had come to rule the mansion in Charleston, where she entertained statesmen, lords, ladies, artists and the gentry. She ordered the finest merchandise from England and France, and tea all the way from China. She ruled her house like a despot, and her only regret in life was that her daughter resembled *her,* and not her dashing husband.

The promise of a fortune should have seen Lygia

well married, but she had read too many books over the years. She refused. She refused the young swains who were not old and ugly, but were only after her money. She refused the fellows who were so old they did not deem her ugly. Her mother had forced misery upon her, just as she did her servants, indentured, most of them, and little better than slaves. But Ellen had never been able to whip or bully Lygia into marriage.

So Red had been blessed with one friend. One who virtually gave her the world, because they shared a passion for books.

Ellen had a way of truly making slaves of her servants. If their time of servitude should come to completion, they were accused of taking something, using something…doing something. And so they owed her more time.

Red had seen many die in her service.

They had died because they had no hope. Their eyes had died long before their bodies had given out. Their spirits had perished. Mortal flesh could do nothing more than follow.

Ellen Fotherington did not hack people to pieces. She did not steal their birthrights. She took what made life most precious: freedom, and their very souls.

In Red's case, she had determined to curry favor by shipping her to France and giving her to a hideous little count with gout and a dozen other wretched diseases to use as he wished. Under lock and key, Red was sent back across the Atlantic.

It was then that Red Robert, the most deadly pirate on the high seas, had been born.

Red lowered her head, inhaling deeply. She steadied herself, and then almost smiled. The captain of a merchantman they had once seized off Savannah had told her that Ellen had died. Slowly. Painfully.

She did believe in God.

And it might have been the only time she had ever believed that God also believed in her, no matter how unChristian such a thought might be. Ellen, who had paraded her entire household to church every Sunday, deserved to be in hell. God could afford to be forgiving; she could not.

Still, Blair Colm, the man who had slain infants in front of her for the sake of expediency, was still alive, a fact that desperately needed to be rectified. God had allowed him to live far too long. God had allowed him to commit far too many atrocities.

God needed her help.

God had helped her create Red Robert, and so Red Robert would now help God rid the world of Blair Colm.

That was one way to look at things, anyway. It was a way of seeing the world that helped her to stay sane and committed to her path.

And now that she had started upon her path, there was no going back.

She would not give up this life—*could* not give up this life—until he was dead.

And so…

On to New Providence.

CHAPTER THREE

New Providence

TO SAY THAT she glittered in the distance would be a stretch. But there she was, big and bawdy, a place where the shouts in the streets were loud enough to be heard from a distance, where many a rogue kept a grand lair in which to exercise his base desires. The wharf was filled with boxes and barrels being loaded and un-loaded; ships lay at anchor in the harbor, small boats plying the shallows back and forth between them and the shore. Women, tall and short, their skin of as many colors as their brightly festooned clothing, walked the muddy roads, past storefronts and taverns and huts, most of them nearly a-tumble.

It was a beautiful day. The ship rested at anchor, gently listing in the bay, beneath a sky that was just kissed by soft white puffs of cloud. The breeze was sweet and clean and caressing, at least out here, where they still lay at ease upon the sea. Logan knew that there were areas of New Providence where little could be called sweet. Slop buckets were tossed out windows, turning the roads to foul mud. And since the populace leaned heavily toward drink, the stale scents of whiskey, rum and beer combined with the fumes of old pipe tobacco to make the resulting stench nauseating.

But from this distance it all looked merely colorful and exciting, even offering a strange charm with its straightforward, no-apology bawdiness.

A hand fell on his shoulder. "It's the isle of thieves, my friend," Brendan said.

"Aye, but honest thieves they be, eh?" Logan said.

"You've been here before?"

"I have."

Brendan stepped back, grinning as he looked at him. "What was a fine gentleman such as yourself doing among the riffraff of this island?"

"Bartering," Logan told him. He hiked his shoulders and let them fall. "I don't recall saying that I was a fine gentleman."

"*Lord* Haggerty?"

"We pronounce it 'laird,'" he told Brendan wearily.

Brendan arched a brow, his easy grin still in place. He was a strange enough fellow himself to be a pirate.

For one thing, his teeth were good.

Then again, it was passing strange that a shipful of burly outcasts should bathe and do laundry, though one of the toughest-looking of the group, Bill Thornton, known to one and all as Peg-leg, had told him that he found it amazing not to have caught the least fever nor been plagued by scabies since he'd taken up with Captain Red. In fact, the man had confessed, he was looking forward to seeing what soaps he might be able to buy in Nassau.

But Brendan…

Interesting man. As interesting as the captain. They were obviously related. Brendan was taller by a good five inches, though the captain—despite the heeled boots—was not short. Brendan stood well over six feet, and had the shoulders of a man who was long accustomed to using his muscles. He was in excellent shape. His features were nowhere near as fine as the captain's, his eyes a paler blue, his jaw far more square. At times, he brooded. When caught in the act, he was quick with a ribald comment or an off-the-cuff remark. He'd shown himself keenly interested in what was going on in the colonies, his interest greatest regarding the more southern cities, such as Charleston and Savannah.

He was friendly. And through that friendliness, Logan had come to know the others. Hagar was like a huge watchdog, a burly man, towering over even Brendan and himself. His hands were massive, his thighs were like tree trunks, and his chest could vie with a barrel. But Hagar, too, was a decent enough fellow, with a fine sense of humor. All seemed to worship the captain, rather than just honor Red Robert.

"As you wish. *Laird* Haggerty, we are about to make shore. Next boat, my good man."

The *Eagle,* as the ship had been dubbed by the pirates, who had changed her name from that which the previous captain had given her, was equipped with two tenders for loading and unloading supplies and cargo, and also boasted two smaller, sleeker ones. The tenders had headed to shore first, with Hagar in charge, and now the first of them was being lowered for those who would follow, Peg-leg, Brendan, Captain Red and Logan, with another huge crewman, Silent Sam, a strapping Iroquois, at the oars.

As the men stood there, ready to make the descent, Red Robert made an appearance in customary attire: high black boots, white shirt, brocade vest, black coat, and plumed, low-riding hat. There was a knife set in the flap in each boot, and a low-riding leather belt carried a blunderbuss and a double-barreled pistol. A sword in a leather sheath hung from the same belt.

Red Robert was prepared.

"Are you ready for New Providence, Laird Haggerty?" Red Robert asked.

"I know New Providence," Logan reminded the pirate captain.

"But it changes, you see," the pirate said. "It changes literally with the wind, for the mood of the town follows that of whichever king of thieves is in port." Red Robert nodded at Brendan.

"My *laird*," Brendan said to Logan, offering a sweeping bow and gesturing him to precede them into the tender.

Logan nimbly crawled over the rail and onto the rope ladder that led down to the small boat, where Silent Sam was already waiting at the oars. Logan jumped the last few feet, feeling the tender rock beneath him, and easily took a seat. He watched as the others followed.

"So, you'll sell my cargo here?" he asked Red and Brendan when they'd taken their seats.

"Every man out there will know I have it soon

enough. Better to rid myself of dangerous riches. Pieces of eight are easier to manage," Red said with a shrug.

"I could have gotten you much more for it elsewhere," Logan said.

"Pity. That's the way it goes," the pirate captain replied.

Logan tried a different tactic. "This is quite a dangerous place to conduct business."

"And have you, despite your current state, come ashore for business?" Red asked.

"I have. But I'm not…" His voice trailed off, and he turned to face the wharf.

"You're not what?" He was startled as Red's gloved hand fell on his knee. The wary anger in the deep blue eyes that met his was disturbing.

"I'm not a pirate."

"The hell you're not," Red said, settling back.

"Well, he's not," Brendan commented.

"Oh, really? He is at least a thief, for was this treasure not already stolen before it came to us?"

Logan stared back at Red but said nothing.

"You do not protest?" Red asked.

"No. Point taken."

The tender drew up to an extension of the wooden dock. Hagar and several of the others were there, waiting.

"Is he here?" Red asked.

Hagar nodded. "Awaiting you at the Cock's Crow."

"Fine. And the cargo?"

"Already at the tavern, Cap'n," Hagar said. "All

know you're the rightful owner, all are considering their bids, should he decide not to buy."

"Fine. Skeleton crew is holding the ship, you know your orders." Red started down the wharf with Brendan. Curious, Logan followed.

Chickens skittered across the dirt road, flapping and clucking as they walked. *"Gardez l'eau!"* someone called out, and they stepped aside in time to miss the contents of a chamber pot. Red strode on with confidence, and Logan noticed men calling out in greeting, all with respectful tips of the hat or touches to the forehead. Red never did more than nod in return.

"Amazing," Logan said to Brendan.

"What's that?"

"I've never seen a group of such derelicts show such respect to another man…even Blackbeard," Logan muttered.

"Red took down the devil, you see," Brendan said quietly.

Logan realized that the other didn't intend for his words to be overheard and answered equally softly.

"The devil?"

"Ever hear of Black Luke?"

Logan frowned. The man had been the terror of the seas, feared and loathed even by other pirates.

Usually a pirate's intent was not to sink a ship or to kill the crew. Ships were valuable. They were usually taken and added to a pirate's fleet. Men were killed only when they refused to surrender, for the captured ships needed crews.

Black Luke had sunk more ships than most men saw in a lifetime. He had never allowed a captured man to live. He had tortured his captives. His men had not voted, as was the pirate way, nor received their fair share of any treasure. There would have been a mutiny, had they not been so terrified for their lives. It had been said that he had eyes in the back of his head. One of his men had once tried to kill him when he had been sleeping. Black Luke had arisen to grab him by the neck and throw him into the sea.

"*Red* killed Black Luke?" Logan asked incredulously.

"Yes."

"How?"

"Talent. And a hell of a lot of luck," Brendan said.

"Were you there?"

Brendan's jaw was as tight as a hangman's noose. "Yes," he said after a moment.

"I can't believe it."

"Believe it."

"I'd heard a rumor that Black Luke was dead, but no one ever seemed to know if it was true, or, if so, how he died," Logan said.

Brendan was staring straight ahead, clearly unwilling to explain.

A door burst open, and a man came flying out of an establishment with peeling white paint and shuttered windows that were open to the day. He was followed by a woman with a mass of wild black hair, bare feet, a low cotton bodice and a multicolored skirt with the hem of a dirty petticoat peeking out from beneath it.

"Take yer filthy paws elsewhere, y' varmint!" she shouted. "My girls are not cheap!"

"Your girls are whores!" the fellow yelled in return.

"But they're not *cheap* whores, and they'll not be taking on the likes of you for nowt. Get away with ye." She paused, a smile splitting her face as she saw Red. "Captain Robert," she said, her tone delighted.

"Aye, Sonya, we're in port. Is Edward about?" Red asked.

"He said ye'd be here. He's a room ready fer yer negotiating in the back. Brendan, poppet," she crooned. "And…what have we here?" she asked with a wink, her gaze moving admiringly over Logan.

She walked up to him quickly with a sway in her steps but stopped short of touching him.

"Why, it's Laird Haggerty," she said with another smile.

That stopped Red, Logan noticed.

"Aye, Sonya. A pleasure," he said, and dipped his hat.

Red was staring at him with an expression that plainly said, *Men. Naturally, he knows the island's harlots.*

Sonya frowned. "You are…sailing…together?" she said incredulously.

"Laird Haggerty is our guest at the moment," Brendan said. His tone, though pleasant enough, indicated that she should ask no more. Then he clapped a hand on Logan's back. "To the rum, eh?" he said.

"To the rum," Logan agreed. He was certain he had

no other choice. But as they entered the noisy, smoke-filled tavern, he could not help but watch Captain Red Robert as the pirate walked toward the rear of the dubious establishment.

"Sonya knows you?" Brendan asked, a wicked gleam in his eye.

"I sail to all the known ports," Logan said.

"Seeking treasure?" Brendan asked skeptically.

"I sell and trade," Logan said, and looked away. "And, of course…every sailor seeks information," he added.

"Information?" Brendan pursued.

"It's wise for all of us to know what happens on the seas. Which…captains sail where."

"Ah. Pity, you didn't hear about our whereabouts, then."

"Pity," Logan agreed.

"LITTLE GIRL! WELCOME!"

The man already entrenched behind one of the tavern's rickety wood tables in the rear corner of the place was huge. His double-breasted jacket was open, as was his cotton shirt, and grandiose lace spilled out over his velvet vest.

Edward Teach, popularly known as Blackbeard, was fond of ostentatious clothing, as strange a contrast as it made with his thick dark hair, formidable size and ruggedly lined features. He was a sensual man, with full lips, large hands and a barrel-deep laugh.

Red cast him a look of baleful warning.

"Ah, think you that the lot of drunks beyond this wall can hear a bloody blessed thing over all their cater-wauling and so-called music and whoring, missy?"

"There are always those who long to topple the successful from power, and you know it," Red reminded him, sliding the chair opposite him out from the table with her foot. As soon as she sat, he reached across the table and took her hands.

"As you wish, Cap'n Red, so it will be. In the darkest of night, in solitude and to the heavens. Cap'n Red. That be that."

"I brought you treasure."

"I steal treasure for a living, as well you know." He arched a brow. "I agreed to meet you here to consider your offer to join forces, not to buy treasure."

She waved a hand in the air. "This is an exceptional treasure."

"Oh?"

"Spanish treasure."

He laughed. "Well, it's sorry I am to say it, but the English have not come up with much treasure. The Spanish are the ones known to be wiping out whole populations and taking what they won't be needing anymore, since they're all dead."

"The English did not claim the lands where gold was to be found," she said. "But, apparently, certain English nobles were willing to pay highly for this treasure. You've seen what I've brought. The pieces and the jewels are exquisite."

"Aye, I've seen what you brought. And it's fine indeed."

"Of course. So you'll offer me negotiable gold for it?"

"I am an exceptional sea thief myself. I can steal my own treasure."

"But this one will cost you half its worth—and not a man to boot. You won't waste a ball or shell, you will not have to let loose a single cannon. You can obtain this rare treasure at an unusually low cost in time, effort and life."

"I like you, and you know it. And I think you should live and take your pretty arse out of all this," he said, nodding seriously.

She smiled. He was one of the most feared men to sail the seas. He knew what she had instinctively fathomed: perception was of far greater value than truth. Not that he hadn't slain his share of opponents, and not that he couldn't be ruthless, but he didn't kill every man he captured, and he was very fond of women. In fact, he had married many of them.

He didn't believe in divorce, but then, his marriages were hardly legal anyway. He was generous and kind with his women, though, and preferred a simple disappearing act to anything more fatal.

"I heard that you chased Blair Colm," she said flatly.

He stared back at her and sighed. "Aye, I saw the man."

She leaned closer. "The ship—or the man himself?"

He leaned in, as well. His beard, in which he took great pride, lay upon the table, with strings tied here and there through it. He liked to light hempen fuses when he went into battle, where he would appear to smoke and nearly burn, an image that filled the hearts of his opponents with terror.

"I saw the man clearly with my spyglass. He has a fine ship. A frigate. He's modified her, but she still can't handle the shallows as a good sloop can. I might have been outgunned, so I did not draw so great a vessel against me. And perhaps he has heard that my reputation is beginning to equal that of any wretch upon the seas, for he had no taste for battle, either. He caught the wind with his mighty sails, and he was gone. He knew he'd find no mercy from me."

"A frigate," Red said. She loved her sloop, but a frigate…was huge. It could carry tons of powder, shot and guns. It could not give chase into the shallows or maneuver narrow channels. But it the open, it was deadly.

"You need to be staying away from him," Teach said.

"You know why I cannot." She met his eyes and asked, "Where did you see him?"

"He was heading north along the coast. I daresay he will hover near the towns and cities where he is honored by the British. Word is that he is looking for you, too. He believes that you stole one of his most valuable possessions."

"How can anyone honor such a man? I do not believe the people can possibly know what a heinous murderer he is."

He caught her hand. "One man kills, and he is a hero. Another kills, and he is a monster. It depends on which side of the battle line one is standing. You are a monster to some. When a man doesn't see something with his own eyes, he doesn't know what is truth, so he believes what becomes legend. Ah, come, girl. The average man wants only to live in peace, so he prays that conflict will not come his way. He is willing to accept the truth of what he is told is the rightful law rather than fight for anything that might disturb his world. Your monster is considered a great military commander by those with whom he does his business in England and the colonies. All anyone there knows is that he helped win the day for King William of Orange and the great empire. Had the war been lost, he would have gone down in history as an ogre. But the English crown was triumphant, and therefore, he is an honored man. Such is history, poppet. It's the deceit I loathe. I don't set out to kill a man. I do so because he is in my way and won't get out of it. My reputation is far worse than my deeds. I prefer scaring a man into surrender. Sadly, there are good men out there ready to die for honor. I don't relish killing them. And unlike Blair Colm, I do not butcher women and children."

"As far as the women go, you just marry them," Red reminded him with a grin.

"Why waste a lovely lass?" he inquired.

"Most of the children turn to piracy."

"I ransom what children I can."

Red looked down, smiling. She wondered what Edward Teach might have become, had he not wound up sailing the high seas. He did have a personal code of ethics.

"Of course."

"And when no one wants them…I do them no harm.

And I'll have you know, they're still hanging children all nice and legal in some ports for offenses not much worse than stealing bread. I'm not a cruel man at all, when you look at the world around me, and see what is done in the name of law and justice."

"I've never said that you were a cruel man. You are a fine captain and swordsman, and you're a wicked shot with a pistol," she said in a tone of genuine compliment. He grunted his pleasure as she continued. "But you are a performer, with that black beard spewing flame and smoke."

He wagged a finger at her. "*You* are the performer." He shook his head. "And to think, if what I heard is true, that a little bit like you killed Black Luke."

She shrugged. "Have you ever seen a tiny insect bite grow infected? Before you know it, a giant roaring fellow is down and dying of fever. Size is not always the deciding factor in a fight."

"Well, I'll take your treasure. I'm quite fond of a number of the trinkets, and I happen to be decently flush with pieces of eight at the moment."

"And what of joining me?" she asked softly.

"That is another matter."

"Oh?"

"You're out for vengeance. I'm out for profit. And how did you come by this treasure, pray tell?"

"I came upon a merchant ship that didn't have a prayer against me."

"So you took the ship?"

She shook her head. "No."

"You sank it?" he asked incredulously.

"No."

"Oh?"

"We parleyed. I now have the captain with me, as my prisoner. He is a Lord Haggerty. Ever hear of the man?" Red asked.

Blackbeard leaned back, grinning. "Aye. I know the fellow. I've met with him in this very tavern."

"But he isn't a pirate."

"No. Neither is he military. He sails a merchant ship."

"Still, he is no outlaw. What was he doing here?" Red demanded.

"Business."

"Treasure?"

Blackbeard laughed. "Nay, poppet. He came to sell what makes a life fine. The finest feather pillows. Silk sheets. Porcelain from China. Tea. Coffee. Apples."

"And he wasn't simply killed in the streets here?" Red asked, amazed.

"I had the opportunity to watch the first time he came. He strode in with his crew, right bold, and when he was challenged, he demanded that he be met man to man. After he bested three of the doughtiest fellows on the isle, I considered challenging him. But, I confess, I was intrigued by his brashness in dropping anchor in the bay, and then stepping foot on land. He was well aware, however, that no quarter would be given to him on the seas if he traveled with merchandise and was caught."

"I didn't give him quarter," Red snapped.

"So he took you in through eloquence as well?" Blackbeard teased.

"He is my prisoner," she said.

"Of course."

She decided to change the subject. "So, I seek revenge, I admit it. And you seek plunder. If we were to go after Blair Colm together—"

"Poppet, give it up."

Red groaned. "Good God, not you, too."

He lifted her chin with his massive forefinger. "I will die on deck. I will die at the point of a sword, or by an enemy volley. That is how it must be. Until then, I will terrorize the sea, I will have a dozen more wives, and I will drink and challenge every man I meet, and mayhap even God. But you...that shouldn't be your life."

"Why not? I would rather die at sea than scrub another floor or be forced to bed some pox-ridden old man or die myself of his venereal disease," she said, deadly serious.

"Ah, but don't you dream of something better?" he queried.

"My dreams are of corpses on a battlefield, the blood of children slain," she said.

He sighed and leaned back. "Sorry, poppet. I'm not suicidal. I won't join my forces to yours, but I will give you gold and buy you rum, eh?"

"Cap'n Blackbeard," she said, determined not to sound disappointed, "I will be honored to lift a glass with you."

He shook his head. "Ah, and you speak like a lady, lass."

"Maybe I was a lady. Once. Past memory, past caring.

God knows, I was so young when the troops came. I remember…"

"Aye?"

"My mother," she said, blushing slightly. "Aye, she was a lady. So softly spoken, so regal…but she is gone, dead and gone, and so is the life I was born to. There is nothing to return to of the life I lived then. But…I have not lost faith in all humanity. There was Lygia."

"Lygia?" he repeated.

"The daughter of the witch who bought my indenture papers from the officer who decided I was worth more alive than dead," she said. "She was ugly as sin, but as sweet and kind as her mother was cold and cruel. We'll drink to her! I imagine she is rich now, with her mother's passing. May she find happiness at last."

"To Lygia. Bless the lass!" he said. "Rich, you say. How ugly was she?"

Red laughed, lifting her glass high. "Quite. But who knows? With enough darkness and enough rum, the ugliest lass may become the fairest. Especially if she is rich. Or so I've heard men say."

He looked at her strangely as he drank his rum.

"Curious…"

"What?"

"That it is *you* who came upon Laird Haggerty."

"Why is that?"

"Ah, poppet. I keep your secrets, but I keep his, as well."

"He has secrets?"

"He has…an agenda."

"And?"

"I just said, I keep a man's secrets."

"Edward…"

"Don't you go wheedling me, girl. I have said all I shall upon that topic. Men come to this tavern for amusement. For whores and for drink. And to listen."

"Listen to what?"

"I've said all I will say."

"But you keep giving me clues!"

"I shall say no more. Drink up."

She tried, but he had made up his mind, and he would say no more. So they drank. She would have her promised gold, and there it would end.

THERE WERE MANY MEN in the shanty tavern so drunk they wouldn't have noticed an earthquake. Some lay on tables in the puddles of their own ale. Whores sat atop the laps of others, mindless of the drunkards snoring nearby. Bodices slipped, hands ran up under skirts and ribald shouting and jokes filled the air, along with the stench of old meat, stale tobacco and unwashed bodies.

Logan turned to Brendan. "Nice place," he commented dryly.

"Aye, and obviously you know it well," Brendan said, his tone equally dry.

Logan shrugged. "You and the captain don't look the type to…appreciate such an establishment," Logan said.

"Nor do you."

"I come for business, then leave."

"There's no legitimate business done here."

Logan had to laugh. "Actually, there is. I certainly

didn't intend to run into a pirate vessel on the high seas, but dealing with pirates on land can be quite profitable."

"And very bad business, as well," Brendan commented, eying Logan carefully. "You do know something about the art of negotiation, my friend. But there are those who don't wish to negotiate. I've met many a fellow who cares nothing for human life. Expediency is what rules. Many a pirate captain would gladly have slit the throat of every man on your crew—or saved steel and bullets and simply tossed them all overboard."

"But not without great loss of life and limb, even if I would have gone down fighting," Logan informed him.

"True enough. So…" Brendan stared at him still. "A man of honor, are you?"

"And your captain's a pirate of honor," Logan returned.

"We'll drink to he—him," Brendan said, lifting his glass.

"What business has the captain with Blackbeard?" Logan asked.

Brendan looked back at him, weighing the risks of sharing information with a captive. "The captain wishes to join forces with Teach."

"With Teach?" Logan was startled. He knew himself that Teach was crafty, but not nearly so cruel as his carefully crafted reputation would have others believe. Teach didn't hesitate to kill when necessary, but he was far more prone to let a man live when possible.

He never relished killing the innocent, as did some fellows on the sea.

Knowing what he knew, Logan couldn't but feel that Captain Red Robert…should not be partnering with the notorious Edward Teach.

His honor urged him to leap up, stride into the private room where the two were meeting and demand Teach unhand the *woman* known as Red Robert. But the impulse was pure insanity, he knew. He had battled Red. She could hold her own. She didn't need nor want his protection.

And, should he attempt to give it, he would no doubt find himself skewered through the heart or the liver, perhaps even castrated, but certainly, in whatever manner, left dead or dying.

Still, it was hard to remain sitting upon the raw wooden stool where he was perched, and warning himself not to be an idiot wasn't much help. Yet surely, if there were something to fear, Brendan would not be sitting beside him so calmly, sipping his ale.

Hagar came up to the bar just then. "Brendan," he said, offering a nod to Logan. "Ye'll be needing to talk to the cap'n. Ship's carpenter has warned, we've got to careen her. Soon."

Brendan frowned, as if warning Hagar to speak softly on such a matter.

Since pirates couldn't simply take their ships into a port and have them dry-docked, it was necessary to take them to a secluded place where they could be "careened," hauled ashore and rolled to each side, so that the hull could be scraped of barnacles and tarred against woodworm. It was a dangerous procedure, for it left both the ship and her crew vulnerable. Most pirates, Logan knew, did only one side of a ship at a time. It was too easy for others to discover that a ship was lying vulnerable, and even if other privateers left her alone, there was always the law to fear. The governors of the various colonies were always pleased to increase their popularity by sending out their naval officers to bring down a pirate, and a hanging was a full day's entertainment for most.

"Aye," Brendan said, and Hagar nodded, aware that it wasn't something Brendan wanted to discuss in their present circumstance.

When Hagar moved on to answer the taunting call of a bare-breasted woman, Logan commented casually, "I take it the fellow has not long been a pirate?"

Brendan ran a finger up and down the heavy glass that held his ale. "You're a decent fellow, Lord Haggerty. If you want to live long and prosper, you shouldn't ask so many questions."

"I've given my word. I won't be trying to escape."

A dry smile curled Brendan's lips. "Aye, but you see, we intend not only to let you live, but to see to it that you are returned to your people, whether there be a fine ransom paid or no. Too much information is not good for a man who will return to the world where the king's law holds sway."

"The king's law," Logan repeated, his tone hinting of bitterness. "There are no doubt good men in that world, but I have never been deceived. Laws are made by those in power. And what men do when they gain power is too often far removed from any law of decency, justice or humanity…far from any law made by God." He turned, then slid from his stool, surprised to see that the door to the private room where Red had been meeting with Blackbeard was open.

"Where is Teach?" he asked Brendan sharply.

Brendan turned. Both the massive Blackbeard and Red were gone. The room was empty of all but its rough wood table and chairs.

"How the hell did we miss a man such as Blackbeard?" Logan asked, unable to believe he had forgotten to pay strict attention.

"He would never harm Red," Brendan said, but he sounded anxious, as well.

He might have been the prisoner, but Logan started for the door. To his surprise, Sonya was suddenly in front of him, setting her palm on his chest, splaying out her fingers.

"Lord Haggerty, don't be in such a hurry," she drawled.

He hesitated, looking at her. He'd never fooled with the whores in this place, though he'd tipped well enough for his drinks. But she knew he wasn't interested in what she had to offer.

She was trying to keep him from leaving.

"Brendan, we need to go," he said sharply.

"What?" Brendan asked.

"Sonya knows something. In fact, I'd say someone paid her to stop us," he said softly, looking into the woman's eyes.

She flushed, lowering her thick lashes.

"Nay, 'tis only that I live by the profits of this place," she said, sounding a little desperate.

"I doubt if any man is brave enough to go after Blackbeard," Logan said. "So who paid you to keep us here so that they could go after Captain Red Robert?"

She stepped away, but he caught her arms and dragged her back.

"Sonya?"

"I don't know!" she snapped. "Some fellow…he gave me gold," she said, as if that would explain everything.

He moved her firmly aside and looked at Brendan. "I haven't figured out what Red Robert is so bent on achieving, nor do I know who or why, but someone is after Red."

Brendan stared at him, then turned toward the door. Logan caught his arm. "We're in this together," he told him quietly. "And may I suggest you call your man Hagar, as well?"

Brendan, face taut, nodded stiffly. For a moment he'd had a reckless look in his eyes. He was a formidable man, tall and muscled, but agile, and his concern would have sent him off without heed, but Logan's words reined in his impulse to rush out alone. He sized Logan up carefully while shouting, "Hagar, gather who you can. We're going after the cap'n. Now!"

They moved out. There were narrow alleys to either side of the tavern, both now dark and menacing, filled with shadows and gloom. Each led into smaller, darker alleys, little craters of blackness that could hide many a sin. Ghostly laundry hung in the darkening mist of the day. A dog howled as the wind picked up, and the screeching cry of a cat sent shivers up Logan's back. A scurrying sound warned them of rats.

The day was no longer what it had been.

The clear sky had gone dark. The breeze had gone chill and brisk, whispering with the coming rain. The clouds overhead billowed and rushed.

A storm was coming, and coming hard.

A perfect shield...

For a surprise attack.

A man stood leaning against one of the supports that held the bar upright, his head on his chest as if he had fallen asleep in a drunken stupor. "Which way?" Logan demanded.

The fellow didn't move.

Logan shook him, and he opened one bleary eye. But Logan didn't believe he was so far gone.

He shook the man harder.

"Which way?" he asked again.

"I don't know."

"Tell me, or I'll slit you from the groin up," Logan said evenly.

"The alley."

"Which alley?" Logan demanded.

"The alley to the left. Cap'n Robert went that way not five minutes past. The...others came out a bit after."

"How many?" Logan demanded.

The man shrugged.

"How many?" Logan repeated, his tone still low, but filled with a menacing promise.

"Eight...ten..."

Brendan was already running into the shadows.

Logan released his hold on the drunk and followed.

And the storm broke.

CHAPTER FOUR

RED KNEW SHE was being followed, and she listened
carefully.

It was exactly what she had expected. No, hoped for.

But as she pretended to saunter along, weaving a bit,
as if she had drunk heavily, she listened hard and
damned the weather. The rain had started. The sky had
threatened that it would come down in buckets, but as
yet, it was just an annoying and continual fall, darkening the world and making it hard for her to listen. She
couldn't tell how many were following. She had as-
sumed it would be just one man. Maybe two. But there
were more than that behind her, she knew.

Blair Colm did not know who she was. He knew
only that the pirate Red Robert had a reputation for
horrible ferocity.

And that Red Robert was looking for him.

And *she* knew that despite his cruelty, Blair Colm
had always been a coward.

When she left Teach, she had seen Sonya taking a
coin from a man. She'd tested it, but Sonya was a busi-
nesswoman—she knew real gold when she saw it. Red
didn't even hate Sonya for the betrayal. The woman's

life was hard. She hated most men. She'd crawled her way to the top of the heap by lifting her skirts for sex in dark corners, turning her face from the putrid breath of unwashed men. Red couldn't hate her.

Maybe she had grown too complacent in her own skills, Red thought now. A sad miscalculation, since she had lost to Logan Haggerty. But he had been different. There was—or usually was—little to fear from other pirates. They passed at sea and saluted one another. They shared dens of iniquity, like the one she had just left. They brawled and wenched and drank, but they seldom picked battles with one another. They shared one bond, the ever-present image of the hangman's noose. No need to battle one another.

But Red had wanted to be followed, for there could have been only one reason for it. And now she knew. Blair Colm had spent a great deal of money to send men out to murder Captain Red Robert.

But now she began to count the footsteps and lament her own reckless determination to see Blair Colm dead. There were at least six men behind her. They would have to be the most drunken, poorest swordsmen in the world to fall victim to her alone. She damned her own stupidity and confidence—her belief that she could best her pursuers in any duel and demand to know from them where Colm was headed now, where he might be found.

She hadn't asked Brendan or any of the men to go with her, for a coward who had taken money to kill would not have followed her if she had been accompanied.

She simply hadn't believed there would be so many.

Ahead, a white sheet billowed as the alley widened, and she hurried beyond it, knowing she had to pick a place to make her stand.

And so she did, checking the line that held the laundry as she held her position, barely daring to breathe, and waited.

She heard the footsteps, coming closer now, moving faster.

"Where's he gone?" came a whisper, just audible in the night.

A flash of lightning illuminated the sky for a split second.

From her vantage point atop a step just beyond the line, Red saw the men. Eight. Two were leaning upon one another, and one of those two carried a bottle of rum. They weren't there to fight; they were just waiting for the kill.

None of them was well-armed. They were debris, she determined. Refuse that had found its way to the island. There was only one—a tall, muscular man, wearing a brace of pistols, his cutlass at the ready— who appeared to offer any real danger. He was bald beneath his sweeping hat, and one of his eyes was made of glass. Though the alley was dark, she could see that; slivers of moonlight caught on it, casting a glint of reflection. That was good. She would attack from the left.

Full darkness seemed to fall when the lightning dimmed. It was time.

With a violent thrust, she set the line of sheets flying. Several of the fellows were toppled immediately. She leapt from the step, her cutlass waving as she strode through the confusion. Easiest first to wind the men into the sheet. More of them fell. But then she discovered a man at her back, ready to skewer her, and when she turned to parry his attack, she saw the bald fellow moving toward her, as well.

From a window above, there was the sound of life at last.

"Glory, what be happening down there?" a woman called out shrilly.

"Battle in the alley! Close the shutters, woman," came a masculine reply.

Lights flickered from above, and were quickly doused. She could hear the slamming of shutters on both sides of the alley now. Apparently none of the residents of this sorry place meant to become embroiled.

She would not be receiving any assistance from them.

She leapt over the tangle of men seeking to free themselves from the sheets just as a third man came at her, followed by a fourth.

She slashed her blade at him, then caught hold of what remained of the laundry line and used it to swing to the far side of the alley to face the remaining three.

She sheathed her cutlass, drew her pistols and fired both simultaneously. She caught one man in the leg and winged the other in the shoulder. But as they fell, two others at last dislodged themselves from the sheets and joined the fray.

Without time to reload, she went for her cutlass again and crouched, finding the knife lodged in the sheath of her left boot. Her aim was swift and sure, and one attacker went down with the blade caught in his shoulder.

Still another fought free of the sheets. It was the sot who had been holding the rum bottle, and he looked sober now. And lethal.

She was dead, she decided, overcome with bitterness and regret. She had expected so little from life. Even so, she had not thought it would end in a filthy alley on a dead man's isle.

"Take the flanks!" the bald man called to his companions.

They planned to back her against the wall, she realized, then come at her from three sides.

She would do as much damage as she could before going down, she resolved.

Would God forgive her for the life she had led? she wondered vaguely.

Was God even there? Where had He been when her family was slain?

But as the bald man walked toward her, taking his time, grinning, she was stunned to hear the loud volley of a gun.

And suddenly the overconfident bald attacker was no longer walking toward her. His one good eye was wide, and then blood burst from his chest, like red tears, for the rain was growing harder, and it mingled with the blood.

The two coming at her from the side froze as the night came alive with shouting and the thunder of footfalls. Brendan was there, Hagar, Peg-leg —and their prisoner.

Her other attackers finally fought free from the sheets, and the wounded men staggered up, desperate to survive. She was left alone at the wall as her attackers and her crew went to battle, deadly and swift. One man tried to run, but Peg-leg was not a man who was prone to mercy. He went after the coward, and the swordplay that ensued was swift. In moments her would-be murderer fell dead in the rush of blood that spewed from his throat.

And then her crew was standing still in the dark alley, looking around, seeking new combatants.

But there were none. They were all on the ground, unmoving.

"Red!" Brendan cried and rushed forward. She saw the terrible inner battle he fought, trying not to reach for her, longing to draw her against him in relief.

"I'm well, good fellows, and I give you my deepest thanks," she said, as Peg-leg clapped her on the shoulder.

"Sorry," he said quickly, realizing how much force he had used. "Aye, but, Cap'n, you were holding your own so fine."

"So fine," Logan Haggerty repeated. She looked at him and could see the contempt in his eyes. She would have died if they hadn't come, no matter how fine she might have been doing. And he… He was a prisoner. But he had come with the others, and had fought well and…loyally?

"Captain Red, what the bloody hell…?" Hagar asked, shaking his head and breaking into her thoughts.

"Let's hope someone is alive to tell the tale," she said, and realized she was shaking. How strange. She hadn't feared death—she really hadn't—though she had hated the fact that she would die before accomplishing her goal. But now…

Now she suddenly knew how badly she wanted to live. Not for vengeance. She wanted to see the sun again, taste the rain, know the feel of the waves beneath her, plunge into a warm sea, read more books…

Feel a human touch that was gentle and tender…

Change that look of contempt upon Logan Haggerty's face.

She gritted her teeth and willed the shaking to stop. She had not come so far to be diminished by the look of a man who had unjustly condemned her as a fool.

"Find someone living in this scramble," she commanded sharply.

As her men moved about the alley, checking the downed men for signs of life, the shutters above them began to open. Lamplight flickered again, making the mist in the air shimmer mysteriously.

"Dead," Hagar announced, rolling over a body.

"This one, too," Peg-leg said.

"Not this one," Logan announced, dragging a man to his feet.

The survivor was skinny, and wore only a shirt, breeches, worn boots and a sword belt that barely clung around his narrow hips. His sword was still sheathed. There wasn't a mark on him.

"Please," he whimpered. "I caused no injury to any of you. I was…I was caught. I was tangled in the sheets."

"You played dead, you mean," Logan said bluntly.

"I…I…"

"Who sent you?" Red demanded.

"I, um…that fellow. The bald man over there. He paid us all. He found us back at Ha'penny Hattie's, and he paid us to follow him down the alley. That's all." He slipped to his knees, looking up beseechingly, his hands folded in desperate prayer. "I was just drinking me rotgut there, I swear it, and the money…as you can see, I'm not a prosperous man."

Red was about to turn away in disgust.

"But you *are* a lying one," Logan said, catching the fellow by his shirt collar and dragging him relentlessly to his feet. "Who paid the bald man?"

"I don't know!" the skinny man screeched.

"You do," Logan said flatly.

"He'll kill me!" their captive implored.

"He's dead," Brendan pointed out.

"No, no, not the bald man…"

"It's all right," Red said. "I know who sent him."

Their captive's eyes were all but bulged out of their skeletal sockets. "I didn't tell you. I didn't tell you!"

"He *may* kill you. I *definitely* will," Logan threatened softly.

Red shook her head. "Don't bother. It was Blair Colm."

Logan stared at her sharply, and she had no idea what was going on in his mind as he watched her. It seemed for a moment as if time had stopped.

"Oh, God!" the skinny man screamed, going limp.

"Is he here? Is he somewhere near here?" Red demanded.

The man slumped down again, but Logan dragged him back up. "Answer the captain," he said.

The fellow just shook his head, moaning.

"Answer," Logan persisted menacingly.

"I—I…no. He's headed north. He's heading up to the Carolinas." He looked up at them at last. "He's…he's no pirate, you know. They welcome him at fancy tables. He's free to sail wherever he chooses and…kill and loot at will. Because he does so for the governors and the Crown, and he's somehow…" He shook his head. He was no longer hoping to hide anything from them. Maybe he wasn't even hoping to survive anymore. "I have never known another man so utterly ruthless and brutal. He's invincible, and you might as well kill me now, and I can only pray you will do so mercifully."

"How will he know you were hired by the bald man?" Red asked.

"He'll know," the terrified man whispered. "There is talk. There is always talk. Tomorrow they will be talking about the fight tonight."

"How did he hire you? Was he here recently?" Brendan demanded.

"No…months ago, he paid the bald man. One-eyed Joe. That's what I heard. And he promised a great reward. That's all I know. I swear it."

"Fight?" Hagar snorted. "Intended execution, more like."

"No one thought Red Robert would go down without taking a few men with him," the fellow said mournfully. "That's why there were so many of us.

This island is hell, my friends, and in hell, people always talk, and there is nowhere to run."

Hagar looked at Red. "We can't take him with us. The man is a coward."

"I was caught in the sheets!" the fellow implored.

"Can't trust him," Peg-leg said.

"We have to kill him," Hagar said.

The man began to moan softly again.

"Oh, shut up," Brendan snapped.

A door opened somewhere nearby. People were beginning to venture out.

"Pick up the good weapons," Red said quietly, and Peg-leg and Hagar hurried to do so, before those who had cowered in their rooms above could come down and, like vultures, prey upon the dead.

Red turned. A man was working at one of the fallen assailant's boots.

"I don't have shoes," he said simply.

Red nodded. "Aye, then, take what you need— except the weapons. The weapons are ours. And see to the bodies."

She started walking slowly away.

"What about him?" Brendan called after her.

She turned, not sure what to say. She couldn't order the man's death. He was right; he was probably a dead man anyway. He was hardly trustworthy. But he couldn't really hurt them in any way.

Before she could open her mouth, he cried out, "Wait! I can cook. I'm a good cook. Meals are wretched at sea, but I can keep meat fresh longer than any man alive, I can mix grog, and I know a recipe that keeps away the scurvy, too."

"Any man can make grog," Hagar said. "Rum, lemon and water."

"But mine is the right combination. Keeps the growth from the water, makes it good and sweet for drinking. And I know spices and herbs. Take me on as a cook. Please," he begged.

"He'll hide in any battle," Hagar warned.

"He can hide down by the guns, then," Red said. "Are you capable of priming and loading a cannon."

"I am."

"What's your name?"

"O'Hara. Jimmy O'Hara. Once an Irishman, never an Orangeman. No country of my own."

She lowered her eyes for a moment. Time had passed, years, and this was a different world….

"Take him on," she said.

When she started walking quickly toward the wharf, unwilling to stay ashore and determined to take the tender back to the ship, she found Brendan by her side.

And Logan Haggerty on the other.

Hagar and Peg-leg brought up the rear, Jimmy O'Hara between them.

And now, even as the rain fell harder, the alley came alive. All those who had cowered in their rooms above were down in the street.

The bodies of the fallen would be picked clean of whatever coins and trinkets, pipes and tobacco, they might have been carrying in their pockets. Boots and clothes, if in any kind of repair, would be stripped. She could only hope the bodies would be buried, as well.

Most probably they would be, she told herself. The residents wouldn't want to live with the smell once the sun rose in the morning and the stench of decay set in.

"Where are you going?" Brendan asked softly. "I thought you had taken rooms."

"The men may enjoy their shore leave, as promised. I'm returning to the ship. Tomorrow we'll take on supplies. Then we'll head north."

"And what about O'Hara?" Brendan asked.

She shrugged. "We'll see if he can cook."

"But he tried to kill you," Brendan reminded her.

"No. He came along because he needed money."

"What if he plans on poisoning us all?" Brendan asked quietly.

She smiled. "Well, we have Lord Haggerty, don't we?"

"Ship's taster," Logan said, not glancing her way.

"Red…" Brendan began.

"Don't worry. I don't believe he's a poisoner. Neither does our good captain," Logan said, then looked at Red at last. "I strive to please."

She stared back at him for a long while. She liked the man, and she hated that she did. Pirates' honor, indeed. Logan had his own code. He could have escaped tonight. Instead, he had fought for her, and fought well and hard.

"Ransom or no, we will set *Laird* Haggerty free in the Carolinas," she said.

He was still staring at her.

"You have earned your freedom," she said simply.

He smiled slowly. "Have I?" he asked softly. "Perhaps I played this game tonight because I knew the other side would lose."

"We'd not have found you without Laird Haggerty," Brendan said. "He threatened Sonya, and then a drunk, to find out where you'd gone. And he was the marksman who killed their leader."

"You might have missed—and gotten me," Red said.

"I don't miss," he assured her.

"Too bad he isn't a pirate, eh?" Brendan said, and stepped between them, slipping an arm around both their shoulders.

"Too bad," she mused dryly.

And too bad that she was.

Better than her other options, she thought, then wished she had never set eyes on Laird Logan Haggerty and his ship.

LOGAN SAT ON DECK, idly tossing bits of dried fish to one of the ship's cats, a tabby he'd grown quite fond of. The animal was called Rat because he was so efficient at ridding the hold of the creatures who would otherwise ravage their food stores. Rat had a harem of females who did his work with him. He was a huge beast, never afraid, and most of the crew steered clear of him. Rat had an affinity for the captain, though, and Red could pick up the cat and he would purr. The animal was as loyal to their captain as the best hound could ever be.

As were her men.

Those who appeared to have come from some kind of finer life, and those who seemed to have been born swabbies.

Peg-leg was in the captain's cabin. Logan had just finished repairing a tear in the mainsail and was about to tar a gap in the hold, but even prisoners were given a luncheon break.

Especially prisoners who had been offered further shore leave but had chosen to return. In fact, being quite fond of his health, he had resisted the entertainments offered by Sonya and her fellows, and had been pleased to return to the ship. Their supplies were being loaded even now, and he had to admit that their new cook, Jimmy O'Hara, seemed to have a good idea of how to buy salt and store meat and the rest of their provisions. He'd tasted the fellow's grog, and it was damned good and even left a fellow with a stable mind. Such a man could be a valuable asset, for he'd heard of far more pirate attacks for simple necessities than he had for gold. Pirates could not put into any port. Meat went bad easily. Weevils tore apart wheat, bread and rice.

A cook—one who could keep food from spoiling aboard ship—was as valuable as a carpenter.

Jimmy had set up a grill on the deck, where he had prepared filets of local fresh fish for the crew. He hadn't lied when he said he had a way with seasonings. Old rice and fresh fish had been turned into a meal fit for a king. If a few weevils had made their way into the rice, they'd been masked by the parsley and saffron the cook had acquired.

Logan been feeling ridiculously content and sated when he had first sat down to play with the cat and rest a spell. But now the lethargy was gone. He was alert, his senses heightened, as he listened to Red discussing her plans with Peg-leg.

"We'll lose the lead we have," Red said.

"Captain, I told you before, we'll be sinking to Davy Jones's locker if we don't take the time to keep our ship afloat," Peg-leg said.

There was silence.

"You should have taken Laird Haggerty's ship," Peg-leg said with a sigh.

"No. This is a finer ship, and better equipped with guns. She was already a pirate vessel."

"Black Luke's vessel," Peg-leg muttered.

"Black Luke's vessel," the captain agreed. "She has speed and guns. She can hide, she can outrun almost anything out there, and she can dare the shallows where most others wouldn't have a prayer. No, she's our ship."

"Then we need to keep her in shape," Peg-leg insisted.

Again there was silence.

Red's regret was almost palpable when she said, "As you wish. But now we're freshly loaded—"

"And I can brace the cargo when we haul her ashore," Peg-leg assured her. "You're not forgetting what you saved me from, Red, and not forgetting that I'd lie down and die—give up me good leg, if need be—for you."

"I know, my friend, I know," Red said softly.

"'Cause you're far from a fool, lass," Peg-leg said.

Lass?

Did the entire crew know that they were sailing beneath a woman? Curious. Most pirates thought it was bad luck to keep a woman aboard. Oh, they had slipped through here and there, those females seeking something they could not find in the regimented life their sex was condemned to on land, but most of the time, if discovered, women were not welcome.

But this was unlike anything he had heard of before.

This was...

Red Robert.

He winced. He had thought that, even if he wasn't blindly, insanely in love with her, he loved Cassandra. He *did* love her. Of course, he loved her. There was everything to love about her. She was beautiful, kind, patient, and she had a gentle personality that was still lively and fun. He enjoyed her company. She was so right for the life he had envisioned for himself....

And at this moment, he couldn't recall her features.

It was insane. He certainly wasn't seduced by any other woman, definitely not a hardened soul masquerading as a pirate. No, it was no masquerade. Red *was* a pirate. He had seen her command her crew. He'd fought her. He knew she could be tough, even ruthless.

But he'd seen her eyes, as well.

He'd seen the pain that slipped past the armor. What caused it?

And why in hell did he care?

He had kept his honor, as she had kept hers. He would be released. She would play out her charade until the day came when she was killed. And by then he would be a free man. With luck, perhaps even a rich one. Ready to marry. To return to Scotland and claim his ancestral home....

Did he really still want that life?

Yes. He owed it to those whose blood had been shed for it. Even if now the possibility of reclaiming his birthright would not come with arms, war and trumpets, but with a simple act of unity, forged because the rightful Scottish queen was the rightful English queen, and parliaments agreed.

His muscles tensed, as they so often did when he let himself think of the past. He understood the hatred. Oddly enough, the man both he and Captain Red so despised would *not* understand.

Blair Colm had no soul. He lived for his own selfish pleasures, for money, power and his creature comforts. His heart was ice, and he had no qualms about killing children, women, the sick, the weak or the elderly.

He enjoyed the pain of others. And despite that, it was true that he could walk about the colonies a free man. If someone were to take a knife to his throat on the streets of Richmond or Charleston, that someone would hang for murder. He'd often thought about that himself, afraid that he would not be able to help himself. That he would attack the man and kill him with his bare hands.

And then hang for it.

Then again, perhaps it was not so hard to believe after all. In his own homeland, women still went to the stake to be burned as witches, and men could still be hanged for stealing a mere loaf of bread or a few coins. As

recently as the "Glorious Revolution" that had raised
William of Orange to the throne of England, they were
hanging witches in the northern American colonies. It
was a harsh world. Perhaps it was no surprise that a
monster like Blair Colm could so freely roam the streets.

Or that pirates could actually have a stronger sense
of honor than so-called honest men.

He wondered why that all seemed so clear to him
now.

They were still anchored outside New Providence.
The storm that had broken last night was gone. The
misting rain had become a deluge during the late hours
of the night, but now the sky was crystal blue and beautiful, and the sea was sweetly calm.

The breeze was gentle, like a soft kiss against his
cheeks.

And all he had thought he knew about the world
had changed.

He wasn't seduced, but he *was* intrigued. Or perhaps obsessed.

No, he told himself. It was no such thing. It was
just curiosity to know what had driven the woman to
such extremes.

"Curiosity killed the cat, so they say," he whispered
softly to Rat. The cat had been extremely cautious of
him at first. Hostile, actually. But Logan had gone out
of his way to befriend the beast.

Why?

Because the cat and the captain were close?

The door to the captain's cabin was opening. Peg-leg
came out, and saw him there. The man's eyes bulged,

and Logan knew Peg-leg was afraid his conversation with Red had been overheard.

Logan laid a finger across his lips.

Peg-leg frowned and quickly closed the door behind him.

"What are you doing here, man?" Peg-leg demanded, but since he was whispering, afraid of being overheard by the captain, his bluster didn't carry much force.

"Resting," Logan said, and smiled.

Peg-leg wagged a finger at him. "You…you didn't hear…" He paused and let out a gruff sigh. "What did you hear?"

"Nothing I didn't already know," Logan said softly.

Peg-leg swore.

"There's no problem," Logan assured him.

"But there is!"

"Oh?"

"Now we have to kill you, and we all like you, Laird Haggerty."

Logan couldn't help but laugh. They weren't going to kill him.

She would never allow it. She hadn't even been able to condemn a man who had been hired to kill her.

"Stop that," Peg-leg implored, still whispering.

Logan sobered; the man was genuinely upset.

"I will never tell. On my soul, on my honor, before God," he swore.

Peg-leg eased back, his balled fists relaxing.

"Do all men aboard know the truth?" Logan asked.

Peg-leg hesitated, then nodded.

"You cannot understand…."

"But I would like to."

Peg-leg looked around. The men in view were busy at simple tasks. Silent Sam was adding a layer of varnish to the mainmast, while two others were busy repairing the portside rail. A man was up in the crow's nest, sanding the wood in preparation for a new coat of paint.

"Come," Peg-leg said.

Logan arched a brow.

"I'll tell you the story of Red Robert."

CHAPTER FIVE

PEG-LEG HAD BEEN gone for several minutes, and still Red continued to stare at the door, frustrated.

She was certain that if they just sailed at full speed...

But she knew she had put off the necessary job of careening the ship because she had been too determined for too long that her quarry was just over the next horizon. It was almost as if he knew where she was and was careful to stay a step ahead.

She frowned, tapping her quill idly upon the desk. It was too bad that Blackbeard would not join her, but she understood that he was a man with his own plan, and that plan was to enrich Edward Teach. She needed to be glad he was her friend.

There was a tap on the door. She instinctively checked her hat, which kept the dark wig she wore fixed securely upon her head. But when she bade the visitor to enter, it was only Brendan.

"Small boats are arriving with supplies," he told her.

"Good. Do you have the manifest?"

"I do."

He handed her the sheet. She smiled again, thinking about Teach. He had given her a hefty quantity of gold.

She had duly purchased a hefty quantity of supplies. Glancing over the sheet, she saw that all she had asked for had been acquired, down to the scented soap. A luxury she could not afford with a prisoner on board, but...

She had sworn she would release him. And she would do so.

The sooner the better, she thought. She felt him watching her far too often. And she was afraid he saw far too clearly. She was also irritated that he continued to prove himself an admirable man.

Brendan cleared his throat.

"What?"

"A letter for you made its way to the tavern."

"Oh?" she said, looking at her cousin, who'd apparently read it already.

"It's an offer of ransom."

Her heart skipped a beat. She was a pirate captain. She had demanded a ransom for Laird Haggerty, and his men had seen to it that a letter had made its way to New Providence. Like letters had probably been sent to Jamaica and every other likely port.

She read the letter quickly.

To the pirate captain known as Red Robert,
Dear Sir,
It has been brought to our attention that you are a man who honors his word. As you are holding something dearer to our hearts than gold, we are glad to believe in his good health and safety. We

are willing to offer whatever price you require for
the safe return of Laird Logan Haggerty. As this
is not a business to be handled through regular
channels, please reply via the same channels as
this missive was received.
Sincerely,
The Right Honorable Lord Horatio Bethany, and,
in the case of my illness, death, or incapacity,
with equal assurance, Lady Cassandra Bethany

She hadn't realized her fingers had tightened on the page until Brendan warned lightly, "You'll rip it."

"I'll write a reply directly, assuring them that there need be no further correspondence, and that the good captain will be released at our earliest convenience."

"What about the ransom?"

She tried to shrug nonchalantly. "We are owed nothing. He proved his valor."

"But they are *offering* a ransom."

"Brendan—"

"The men will think you have grown soft."

"The men will remember how often I save their lives."

"Red, let's face it. We're really not in the business of taking ships and treasure, but even so, you have a reputation to uphold."

"And let my reputation be that I honor a man of honor. Pirate or no."

Brendan rolled his eyes. "I knew *I* should have been captain." She looked at him, arching a brow. "All right, cousin, I admit you saved my life. But you must admit that I was doing well, thanks to Lygia."

He shrugged. "Write your letter, then, so it can be left."

Brendan closed the door as he left the master's cabin. Black Luke's cabin, once upon a time.

But, when he was gone, she didn't dwell on Black Luke. She looked at the letter, and her fingers trembled. The letter had been written with love. Logan Haggerty had a home, a safe port, a place where he was esteemed and admired. He was not a man who would ever hang.

He had...

Cassandra.

Of course he did. No man who looked as he did could be without a sweetheart.

Impatiently, she dipped her plume into the ink and began to write. She would do as she had promised, as she should.

But it hurt. And she was angry with herself for that, because she was a realist, and she knew all about the harsh truths of life.

Still, she couldn't help wondering. Did he love his no-doubt adoring Cassandra in return? Did he dream of her by night, and in those dreams, did he touch her and hold her tenderly in his arms?

What would life be like if she knew such tenderness? With even just a sweet whispered hint of passion... of love?

His was a world she could never know. She must write the letter. Get the man off her ship. Remember her quest...

"THE SEA IS A HARSH and cruel mistress, we all know that, lad," Peg-leg said, looking out over the bow.

It was true, Logan thought. He knew the sea, knew it could be hard, cold and treacherous. But at the moment, it couldn't have been more beautiful. At a distance, Nassau, New Providence, even looked enchanting, the colorful shanties near the shore, the rise and fall of the landscape beyond.

"And not just the sea, but the men who sail her, as well," Peg-leg said.

Logan turned, crossed his arms over his chest, leaned back against the rail and stared at Peg-leg. "The *men?*" he asked politely. They were, after all, discussing, Captain Red Robert.

Peg-leg appeared distressed.

"Your tale?" Logan prompted. "What made Red a pirate?"

Peg-leg sighed deeply. He looked toward the captain's cabin, clearly afraid he had given her away. His look was protective and sad; he deeply admired his captain.

"I told you, I already knew Red was a woman. I will be far more likely to remember at all times to keep the secret if I can truly understand it," Logan told him.

Another sigh followed.

"Peg-leg?"

Peg-leg looked off into the distance, as if he were seeing a different time and a different place.

"I was working a merchantman at the time. The ship was under hire by a certain Lady Ellen Fotherington. Do you know the name?" Peg-leg asked him.

Surprised, Logan hesitated.

"Yes, mean old broomstick of a woman," he admitted at last. "Her husband was a fine enough man. I met him upon many an occasion in a tavern by the water in Charleston. But he died when I was young, and I met her but once or twice. She passed away in the last year, so I heard."

Peg-leg wagged a finger at him. "Goes to show, perhaps, 'tis true that only the good die young, because she was not a good woman and, sadly, she did not die young."

"She is dead now," Logan said pragmatically.

"Well, 'tis a long story, but the short of it is that she had rights over the future of a certain young woman. Our Red. Well, no matter how rich and high that wretched Lady Fotherington might have been, she always wanted to be richer. Oh, she was a harridan, and I'm glad you met her, because elsewise, I might not have the power to explain properly."

Logan knew that Lady Fotherington had been fond of taking on indentured servants, although she owned slaves, too. But she knew how to turn her indentured servants into slaves, as well, creating debts they must also pay, accusing them of some crime. Logan had seen it done all too often. Indeed, had he not found himself, by chance and good fortune, in the home of such a man as Master George Delaney, he himself might have suffered a similar fate before reaching his majority. He'd been bitter and resentful, fighting like a wild cat, when he'd first arrived in the colonies; only Delaney's kindness had changed his course in life.

"Red was a prisoner on this particular merchant-man, which was captained by a fellow named Nimsby. Nimsby was an evil man, and he was cheap," Peg-leg continued. "He was hard on his crew, though, quick to take the cat-o'-nine-tails to the back of any man who committed any infraction. He never traveled with enough men—and he never traveled with enough guns. He'd been known to carry human cargo from Africa, and he allowed little room for anything that could not make him money. I was in his employ because I'd been taken off another ship and it was sign on with Captain Nimsby or…well, take my chance with a trial and the hangman. I've not often seen trials go well in the colonies. On this particular trip, Nimsby was carrying molasses and a few other staples home to mother England before going south to Africa, then east to the Caribbean and back to Charleston again, his customary route. He'd been given quite a fair sum by Lady Fotherington to deliver one particular piece of cargo to France—that being the woman you now know as Red Robert. It was on leaving Charleston, just out of the shipping lanes, that we were beset."

"By pirates?" Logan queried.

"By pirates led by a beast," Peg-leg assured him.

"A crew captained by Black Luke?"

Peg-leg nodded gravely. "The very same. I had seen Red, of course, but barely. She'd been brought aboard by two burly fellows who saw her into the captain's cabin, and she was kept there under lock and key."

"Did this Nimsby…assault her in any way?" Logan asked, furious at the thought.

"Oh, no. Nimsby was far too fond of gold to go against the Lady Fotherington's wishes. Red was destined for an aging French count."

"Who?" Logan inquired curiously.

"Le Comte de Veille."

Logan grimaced. The fellow had just perished at eighty-plus. He had gone through several wives, dozens of mistresses and, by reputation at least, hundreds of whores. He was said to have been pock-marked so deeply that he was barely recognizable as human, unable to walk and suffering the insanity of late-stage syphilis.

"Was she a relative? Perhaps a niece?"

"No. She was *bought*. She was meant for the bed of the Comte de Veille," Peg-leg said, horrified.

Logan shuddered, thanking God that Red had escaped such a fate. "Go on. How did a Frenchman's…mistress, locked in a cabin, become the pirate Red Robert?"

"Desperation," Peg-leg said. "And love," he added sadly.

"She was in love?" Logan asked with a frown.

"Young master Brendan is her cousin. Surely you have discerned that they are related," Peg-leg said.

Logan nodded. "She…wasn't in love with her cousin, was she?"

Peg-leg's look of absolute indignation was humbling.

"They'd been together as children, working in the household of Lady Fotherington. He'd been sent to fetch and carry and work on the merchantman, but he was an able and quick lad, and some of the crew grew quickly fond of him. He had a knack with a sword. He said there had been a groom back in the colonies who had enjoyed teaching the children the art of fencing when the old harridan was about on other business. There was a daughter, you see, Lygia. And she was the very soul of kindness. When her mother wasn't at home, she saw to it that all the children received some special treat, the slaves and the indentured servants both. She loved fencing and reading and the like, so…young Brendan knew how to handle a sword."

"And then…?"

"Then bad went to worse," Peg-leg assured him.

"Pray, go on."

Peg-leg sighed. "Black Luke bore down upon us. Nimsby felt he had nothing to fear, as he was good friends with a man named Blair Colm. He—"

"I know the name," Logan interrupted curtly. "And not only because he sent those men after Red."

"Well, then, you know he is known to travel with plenty of guns, and any pirate who has ventured to attack him has gone to the depths of the sea or had his head parted from his shoulders. His friendship with Nimsby had saved the man before, but this time Nimsby had placed himself in the path of Black Luke. Black Luke was a pirate's pirate. He didn't care who Nimsby knew, nor did he intend to sink the merchant-man. He wanted to seize her, and all who were aboard." Peg-leg took a deep breath, then went on. "When the firing started, Nimsby was preoccupied. I took it upon myself to unlock the master's cabin, and I warned the girl within that we were under attack by a pirate, and that she must look to herself. Nimsby was killed almost immediately, when cannon fire brought down the mizzenmast. Then Black Luke boarded, and we were all a-fightin' for our lives. Young Brendan was proving himself such an able combatant that he was cornered by several of the vermin from the pirate ship, and then Black Luke himself. All looked bleak indeed, I can tell you. Then, suddenly, this force of fury comes streaking out of the captain's cabin, cutlass waving madly. It all happened so fast.... There was a whir of motion, and then suddenly Black Luke was dead. He'd turned and roared he was about to cut down a little louse, thinking that Red was the man she'd dressed up to be. But he underestimated her. She'd taken her swing before he could finish his words.

"That's what I meant by love. The brigand had been about to kill her cousin, and that had given her the strength she needed. I think she was as stunned as anyone. Everyone just went still. When we looked around…there were mostly dead folks, and the ship was sinking. Without Black Luke, the pirates were suddenly trying to make it back to their own ship, but there weren't enough of them left to man her. Suddenly the girl who had been locked in the captain's cabin and come out like the wrath of God was shouting orders. The pirates who weren't dead believed that Black Luke had been slain by another pirate held captive in the captain's cabin, and they were set into the merchantman's longboats to make it to shore if they could. And Red took over this ship, just as we have her now.

Those of us on the crew who survived…Silent Sam, myself…and a few others, well, we swore to honor her, and so did Hagar, who'd been sent to tend to her and Brendan by Lady Fotherington. We'd been serving the likes of the wretched Nimsby and nearly died because he'd not had enough guns. It…was easy to serve her. And to keep her secret."

"So…none of you were pirates before?"

"The cooper and the ship's carpenter…they were from Black Luke's ship. But they were both grateful not be serving beneath Black Luke, and they proved to be fine men. So…we started sailing the seas. We made up a dandy flag, and we all vowed to go by the pirates' articles, as set down years ago by Bartholomew Roberts. We've not needed to fight near as often as you might think. Folks usually give over to a pirate ship with surprising speed.

"You must never give her away, Laird Haggerty. Never. I'd have to kill you," Peg-leg assured him, adding softly, "Or die trying, at the very least."

"I would never give her away."

"Even once you've been ransomed yourself?"

"I would never give her away. I swear," he vowed.

"Thank God," Peg-leg said, and scratched his head. "I'm not so sure I *could* kill you. You're pretty handy with a blade yourself. And you've never been a-pirating, eh?"

"Maybe we're all pirates in a way, Peg-leg, seeking something we don't have."

"Now what would a laird need with pirating ways?"

"A good question. I might ask a similar one. I don't see our captain as a greedy vixen sailing the seas for riches," he said.

Peg-leg shrugged, turning away.

"What is her argument with Blair Colm?" Logan asked the man's back.

"That is a tale I cannot tell," Peg-leg turned and said solemnly.

"And why not?"

"Because I do not know it," Peg-leg said. "You see, young laird, I did not say that I *would* not tell you, only that I *cannot.*"

"If she is after him, I would gladly sail with her until he is found," Logan said.

Peg-leg studied him a long moment. "And glad I'd be to fight at your side, Laird Haggerty. But I believe she intends to set you free as soon as it might be done."

"But the ship needs careening," Logan said.

Peg-leg actually blushed a furious shade of red. "She's a good ship," he muttered, embarrassed that he had most certainly been overheard.

"So…it will be a while," Logan said.

"So it will. Who knows what may come?" Peg-leg said. "The sea…always a wicked mistress, eh? Tempting with her beauty and her promise, deadly in her vengeance."

Was he truly speaking of the sea? Logan wondered, and thought of their captain instead. Her eyes were just as Peg-leg had just described the water they sailed. As blue as a clear sky at times, then deep and indigo, roiling like a tempest at others.

"Today the ocean is at peace," Peg-leg said gratefully.

"Aye. Today…she is serene and lovely. Gentle and sweet," Logan said. What had he been thinking? Red Robert was never at peace. She was always torn within, so it seemed.

Peg-leg studied him seriously once again. "Well, we shall see."

"So we shall," Logan agreed.

THE CARGO HOLD was filled, and the anchor was raised. The breeze was picking up, filling the majestic sails, and the ship set out to sea as if she rode above the clouds.

He worked the mainsail with Silent Sam and Peg-leg at his side. At the bow, Red Robert stood, hands clasped behind her back, as she faced the wind. She had learned to ride the waves, and she swayed ever so slightly, as if she were one with the ship. She didn't shout out orders; she spoke them to Brendan, who called them out to the crew. They were headed north, on a path that would eventually lead them up the Florida coast to Georgia, and then to the outer banks of the Carolinas. Logan was convinced at first that she didn't intend to bend to Peg-leg's plea that they careen the ship for cleaning, but as they neared northern Florida, he began to recognize a number of the islands, and he realized she must know of some safe haven where they could go to make the necessary repairs.

The day had been perfect. It wasn't until nightfall that Logan first felt the shift in the wind, which came with a sudden cooling. The day had been hot, the heat eased only by the sweet rush of the breeze. At dusk, he felt the difference, and he saw that several of the men seemed to notice something amiss, as well.

He was pondering the weather when he found Brendan at his side.

"Captain Red would have a word with you, Laird Haggerty," Brendan told him.

"Oh?"

"Captain's cabin."

He nodded. He had just donned his coat against the chill, and he followed Brendan with his shirt duly tucked, his hair queued, his vest in order and his boots polished. He entered her cabin when she bade him to and stood before her desk, waiting for her to look up. While he stood there, he examined the books lining the shelves. Most were sea charts, logs and navigational manuals, but there were works of fiction, as well. He couldn't help but wonder if Red hadn't added to the library that had once been Black Luke's.

"It has been drawn to my unhappy attention that the ship must receive maintenance," Red said without looking up. She dipped her quill into the ink and continued writing in what appeared to be a log.

"So it goes with ships," he said.

She glanced up at that. "I'm assuming, Laird Haggerty, that you have brought your ships into dry dock, but I'm afraid that's not a possibility for us, as you can well imagine. I had hoped to see you safely set upon an island in the Outer Banks within days, but I'm afraid that will be out of the question until we've completed repairs."

"I'm at your disposal," he replied with dry humor.

"Hmm," Red murmured, returning to her writing. "I received a letter today. A Lord Bethany—and a Lady Cassandra Bethany—have offered to pay for your safe return."

Logan didn't know why he found that information so disheartening.

"They are good people," he said simply.

"I left a reply. Good people are apparently not above finding those who are willing to enter pirate towns. The letter came through the Cock's Crow."

He smiled slightly at that. "Captain, I have been in that tavern before, as you know. I am glad that you will receive the ransom."

Red studied him for a moment. "I left a reply that you would be left safely ashore. We are asking no ransom."

"That's quite generous of you."

"You are apparently quite dear to Lord Bethany—and his daughter. I thought you should know."

It was curious that she seemed to be expecting something from him.

He was silent for a moment. "Thank you," he said. It was almost a question.

"Lady Cassandra Bethany. Is she your fiancée?" she asked. The tone was casual, as she set quill to ink once again.

"Not at this time."

Red looked up again. "Ah. Perhaps your beloved?"

"A very dear friend."

"A proper young lady?"

"Quite proper, yes. Why do you ask?"

Red set down the quill and sat back, a half smile curving her lips. "I'm sorry. I'm just imagining your life. The drawing rooms, the elegance. A proper young woman. Ah, but proper can mean so many things among the wealthy. Proper—she's rich. Proper—she has a title. A proper marriage would no doubt provide a wonderful advancement in your social status."

The words were like nails raking down his back. *Proper* could be all those things. But if he'd had his own doubts about sincerely being *in* love, rather than feeling an infatuation and an affection for someone, the taunting words of the captain were like knife cuts against his soul. He found himself taking a step closer to her desk and leaning both hands upon it. "She is proper in every way, Captain Robert."

Red laughed suddenly. "Does that mean she's as ugly as sin?"

He shook his head. He could be honest. "No. She's a striking beauty, truly. Eyes like emeralds, and hair as blond and rich as gold. That is the truth. But even did she not have such a lovely visage, it wouldn't matter. She has a certain purity of heart, a sweet humor, and is ever willing to help anyone downtrodden or in danger. There is truly nothing ill to be said of her."

"Well, I hope you will both be very happy. It sounds as if you make a perfect match. I had not previously imagined such a thing could really be, I admit," Red said, and the laughter was gone. There was no taunt to the words.

Yes, we *should* be perfect together, he thought.

And yet…

What was missing? Whatever it was, he had come to realize that Cassandra certainly deserved far more than what he could give, something that had nothing to do with lands or riches.

"That's all, Laird Haggerty," Red said.

"Pardon?"

"That's all. You may leave."

He bowed and exited the cabin. As he closed the door, he felt the further drop in temperature and realized with a certainty that a storm was coming.

In the distance, he could see a sheet of rain across the eastern sky. He didn't know how many miles off the storm was, but it was going to be severe when it arrived.

Brendan was striding toward him with a frown furrowing his brow.

He nodded curtly to Logan; he was anxious to reach the captain's cabin.

"A storm is coming," Logan said.

"Aye."

"We need to lower the sails."

"Aye."

Red had sensed the change from inside her cabin; she emerged now and stood by the door, as if smelling the air and feeling the direction of the breeze, which seemed to have gone suddenly still.

"It's coming from the east," Logan said.

"I'll order the sails brought down," Brendan said.

"No, not yet. Catch what wind we have. Isla Blanca is not far," Red said. "If we can make her cove, it will be a safer place than we might find here or by pushing out to the open sea."

"You can't outrun what's coming," Logan warned.

She gazed at him, aggravated. "I don't intend to attempt to outrun the storm, merely bring the ship into more protected waters. Brendan, take the helm and cut a hard course."

He nodded.

"And call the hands," Red said quietly.

"All hands on deck!" Brendan shouted.

There was a scurrying sound, footfalls upon the planks, as the crew gathered from their tasks.

"Batten her down!" Red ordered. "All cargo, no matter how small, goes below. Extra rigging, gear, anything that might blow or roll overboard…down below."

At that moment, an eerie silence fell over them, as if nature herself had stilled.

Logan knew that silence, just as the crew did, and knew it well. It was the calm that came just before the fury and tumult of a storm.

"See to the small rigging, Logan," Brendan ordered on his way to take the helm from Silent Sam.

"Check your setting. Hard west, northwest," Red ordered.

Amazingly, despite the deadened wind that was just a wicked tease before the gale, Red's orders brought them whipping hard toward the shallow waters. There were many islands here, Logan knew.

And treacherous sandbars as well.

At least they were far north of the reefs that might have torn apart the hull; if they could ride the waves without breaking up, they could weather the coming storm. As he wound and stored heavy ropes and canvas, he had to admire the seamanship of the pirate captain.

"Lower all sails!" Red called out when they reached the cove. Hagar took up her order, and it was roared about the ship.

Logan raced to join the men. Muscles bulged on massive, hardworking forearms as the crew set about the task. From the crow's nest, a crewman shouted down, "She's on us!"

Red stood at the stern then, her spyglass in her hands. Hagar was near, repeating her orders as she called them out.

"Down from the lookout, Davy!" the big man ordered.

And then the rain began.

It came with a sudden rage, along with the wind, which blew so hard it seemed the rain rose from the sea and tore at them horizontally. It stung like a swarm of bees. It was like being raked over and over again by massive talons.

"Lash yourselves to the mast!" Red yelled, but it was an unnecessary order, for the crew seemed to know by instinct that the time had come when the ship was at the mercy of the waves, and themselves with her.

Brendan tied himself to the wheel, doing his best to keep the ship perpendicular to the wind and avoid being hit broadside by the tremendous force of the sea and the storm. But despite their best efforts, a rope broke from the mainmast and came flying down toward Brendan, the large and lethal steel grommet at the end heading straight for his head.

Red saw what was happening. She hadn't tied herself to the ship yet, and she went running.

As Logan and Hagar did.

Logan launched himself at the rope, catching it just seconds before it could complete its downward arc. He flew with it and crashed into Brendan himself. The breath was knocked from them both, but the disaster had been averted.

Hagar, however, had been pitched, helpless, to the side of the ship just as she had taken a hard roll.

"No!" Logan heard Red's roar of denial, and saw her go flying after the man as he threatened to roll off the starboard side. She caught hold of him by the belt, and as the ship rose again and pitched in the opposite direction, she and Hagar rolled back to safety.

But the wind was wicked and ruthless.

It shrieked like a banshee, tearing around the naked masts, swirling the sea to further violence. The ship rolled hard again, and this time it was Red who was helpless as she was picked up by the storm and flung straight over the side.

Logan let out a shrill scream of anger, fear and fury that rose even above the howling of the wind.

He had to move in split seconds, even knowing that in this sea, with these waves, he was surely committing suicide with no chance of finding, much less saving, her.

But he had no choice.

He stripped off his coat as he raced across the deck, leapt to the rail and plunged into the vortex below.

PERHAPS IT WOULD be a welcome grave, Red thought.

She could swim, could even buck strong waves, and she knew about currents and giving herself over to the power of the ocean, floating to save her strength, to save her breath....

But there seemed to be no top and no bottom to the water. There was no wave that offered the promise of carrying her to shore. There was no air, no sky, no *surface*. She was plunging down....

She was dead, or soon would be....

She could hear it all again. The screams of the children. She could see it all again. The endless spill of blood.

No, she told herself. The scream was the wind.

The blood was the sea.

Then there were arms around her. Surely they belonged to those who now were only vague memories, whispers of what love and family could be. There was a world beyond, and she had to make it through this maelstrom to reach them where they waited for her.

"Breathe!"

Something vised violently about her chest. She spat out seawater, and her lungs instinctively dragged in huge drafts of air, but even the air was wet, and she gasped and choked. The pain was so great that she longed to slip below the cold surface again and let the water cradle her and draw her under.

"Breathe, damn you! Live!"

She gulped in air again. She was being dragged. Dragged through the water and the waves. She tried to breathe, but the waves were sweeping over her again and again.

"Hold on!"

Hold on? To what?

Then she could feel something. Something solid. Wood. And it was holding her above the waves. She felt someone tugging at her feet, and suddenly she wasn't being pulled down so heavily. She felt…her toes. Her boots were gone. And she heard a voice. "The coat… dammit, it has to go. We need to lighten you up…"

She felt like laughing. She wasn't a ship! But something logical in the back of her mind fought against the shock that had seized her, and she knew the boots would have dragged her down, and she had to hold on and kick to stay afloat.

The ghosts of the dead had *not* come for her….

She was dimly aware of Logan Haggerty's face, his dark hair plastered to his forehead, his amber eyes like strange beacons of fire, anger and determination.

"Hold on," he commanded again.

So she did, managing to wrest herself half out of the water, clinging to what she saw now was a barrel. He was next to her, one arm around her, the other clinging to the barrel literally for dear life.

The world was dark, the sea a swirling vortex from which there could be no salvation. The rain lashed at them, so cold, until she felt as if her fingers could grip no more…

Then…

The banshee wail began to fade.

"Kick!" he ordered.

And she tried, oh, God, she tried….

And after that…

What seemed hours later, she felt her feet scrape against sand. Then she was standing, struggling, the waves lapping around her feet….

She staggered forward. The world was still wet and dark and cold.

She fell.

But she fell on solid ground.

CHAPTER SIX

LOGAN REGAINED CONSCIOUSNESS SLOWLY.

First he heard the waves, gentle now, easing up on the shore. There was a cadence to them, a rhythm. It was pleasant, inducing him to close his eyes again and sleep....

But then he felt the sand, gritty beneath his cheek and in his clothing, caked along his jaw.

And there was a breeze. Something balmy, such a pleasant touch, inducing him to forget everything else, to fall asleep and dream.

There was the sun. Growing warm overhead...

Suddenly his eyes flew open, and all the force and fury and desperation of the storm returned to him. He remembered.

Red going over the side.

Brendan screaming.

And himself...

Following her into that storm-tossed hell.

There had never been a question. He remembered diving over the rail, praying that a sudden wave wouldn't tilt the ship over on top of him, that he wouldn't crack his head wide open before he had a chance to save her.

And then…

The water. Deep and churning. Violent. He had dived deep, terrified that he would never find her. But he had, and then he had surfaced and found the barrel, and somehow they had both ridden it as the storm raged and finally passed. He had talked to her throughout, but she hadn't heard him. And he could remember seeing land at last, and kicking for it with the tail end of his strength…

Well, he had evidently made it. He was alive, judging by the sunshine, the breeze and the gritty sand.

He sat up.

His shirt was sodden, molded to his body. His boots were gone. He had one stocking left. He vaguely remembered struggling out of his coat and vest. And Red… He had gotten rid of her boots, as well, tried to rid her of what weight he could. And she…

Panic suddenly locked his throat and soul.

Where was she?

He struggled up, looking around.

Where the hell was she?

He looked down the beach and saw the broken barrel that had been their salvation. There was other flotsam and jetsam on the shore, as well.

But he didn't see Red.

He started running barefoot down the beach, his heart pounding furiously as he raced past the barrel and skidded to a stop.

He exhaled, shaking and falling to his knees at her side. She lay there, clad much as he was himself, torn white shirt, ripped breeches and, amazingly, both stockings. With the wig gone, her eyes closed, her features pale, perfect and fragile, and the radiant color of her hair, she appeared as delicate as a kitten.

His throat seemed to close again.

Was she alive?

He reached out and touched her throat, seeking a pulse.

It was there.

As her eyelids began to flutter, he pulled back his trembling fingers.

Her eyes opened.

She stared at him in confusion. For a moment her gaze was innocent and questioning....

Then she bolted up, staring at him in horror, as her hand flew to her head.

She was looking for that stupid wig.

He could see in her eyes as it all came back to her.

The storm...

Going overboard...

Then...

"You!" she gasped.

He didn't know what to say. He hadn't expected her to fall all over him with gratitude for saving her life, but he hadn't expected such pure horror, either.

"Me," he said, crossing his arms over his chest. "The storm, the ship...remember? Then there was me— jumping overboard to save you."

"You...you know who I am."

She backed away from him.

"Don't be ridiculous," he snapped. "Of course I know who you are. Did you hear what I said? Yes, it's me. The man who jumped overboard to save your hide!"

She backed away again.

"I...I am a pirate. I am Red Robert!"

"Fine, you're Red Robert. Now stop worrying about the fact that you've lost your wig and you've very evidently a woman. This may shock you, but I was too busy being concerned about whether you *lived or died* to care much one way or the other!"

She stood very tall and wary, and clutched her arms around herself, as if that would somehow disguise her again.

"Where are we?" she asked suspiciously.

"On a beach."

"The ship?"

"I don't know—I dived in after you."

"You didn't have to," she informed him.

"Yes, I did."

"The others?" she asked, her eyes downcast with fear for her crew.

"She's a good ship. They probably rode it out."

"They'll come back for us."

"We can hope. We can also hope they'll figure out where we washed ashore."

"And now you know," she said miserably.

He couldn't help but laugh.

"*Now* I know?"

She stared at him, stunned.

"Of course I know. I knew all along."

"You did?" she demanded.

He stared back at her, irritated. His heart had practically broken when he had thought she'd died, and now this.

"Excuse me," he said. "I'm going to take a walk. I'm going to try to figure out if there's any water on this island."

He turned, heading into the tangle of palms and brush that grew not far from the shore. Hopefully that abundance of growth meant there was fresh water somewhere.

His back was to her, but he could feel her staring after him as he walked. The sand was still cool from the night before and the battering of the storm. He saw that the trees were coconut palms, so at the least they could drink coconut milk and eat the coconut meat.

He heard her when she came racing up behind him.

"You *knew?*" she repeated furiously.

"Of course," he said, moving into the shade of the palm trees.

"From the beginning?" she demanded.

"Yes," he said. It wasn't a complete lie.

She caught hold of his shirt, spinning him around. "That first day on the ship. The first day. When you fought me and slashed my cheek. You knew *then?*"

"Yes." Well, he'd known *something* wasn't quite right.

"Bastard!"

The word stunned him. He stood dead still and stared at her coldly.

"You chose to fight, and you fought like a hellion," he reminded her.

It didn't help the situation.

"Bastard," she repeated.

He shrugged, walked on, then turned back. "Look, we need to find water and—"

To his amazement, she charged him. And to his deep humiliation, he wasn't prepared. He went over backward, with her on top of him, her fists pummeling wildly. Luckily for him, she was so furious that she wasn't being her usual cool and calculating self, and her energy was quickly spent as he went for her flailing arms, trying to avert serious physical harm.

"Of all the despicable, horrid, obnoxious, wretched men in the universe…!"

She stopped raging at him only because she ran out of breath. He took advantage of the moment to gain the edge, clutching her arms and rolling her over so that he was on top, straddling her and pinning her to the sand.

She never stopped thinking, planning, conniving. He could see it in her eyes. Knowing she was wasting her efforts, she went dead still and stared up at him with twin blue beacons of blazing fury. She seemed beaten, but he knew her better.

She was just waiting for a hint of weakness, of vulnerability, on his part. He wasn't going to give it.

"I'm despicable? Because you're playing such a dangerous game?"

Her eyes narrowed with an ever greater anger. "This is no game," she assured him.

"You are no pirate."

To his amazement, her anger seemed to fade, but her demeanor was still icy. "I'm afraid that I am very much a pirate."

"The great and fearsome Red Robert?" he mocked.

"I took down Black Luke," she reminded him.

"I heard about that—*all* about that."

Her eyes widened then, and she cursed.

Like a pirate.

"Which one of those demented idiots told you... anything?" she demanded.

He had to hand it to her. One would have thought she was the one wielding the power.

"The cat sang," he told her.

She cursed again and struggled then.

"Stop it!" he told her. "Stop fighting and listen to me. You are amazing and incredible. What you did...it was foolhardy, but it was also brilliant and valiant, and you saved yourself and a lot of men. But...do you know what will happen eventually?" he asked softly.

"I cannot come to a worse end than what was intended for me."

He couldn't help but grin, and he relaxed back on his haunches, still wary that she might fly into another rage and attack, and then grew serious. "But you can stop now," he assured her. "The wretched woman who held your indenture papers is dead."

She stared back at him without comment.

"You can live an...an honest life."

She shook her head. "It's too late. I can't turn back."

"You could work for me," he said.

"As what? Your scullery maid?" she asked, and her fists started flying again.

"I didn't say that," he told her.

"Oh, I should perhaps be your mistress? Or merely your whore?"

"Never. I intend to honor the woman I marry."

She went still, staring at him. For a moment he thought there was a sheen of dampness—maybe even tears?—in her eyes.

Then she struck out at him again, and it was all he could do to stop her.

"Bobbie!" he said. The name he'd heard Brendan use with such affection came easily to his lips. "For the love of God, I don't want to see you at the end of a hangman's noose. Or at the mercy of such a man as Blair Colm."

She went dead still.

What was it about Blair Colm that upset her so? he wondered.

Had she already been at his mercy?

But she was alive....

"I am what I am," she said primly. "And that is a pirate. And now, if you would get off me, I would greatly appreciate it."

He slowly relaxed, but he didn't let go of her wrists. "I don't know."

"What do you mean, you don't know?"

"Are you going to hit me again?"

"You're worried that I'm going to hit you again? You sound like a little girl," she snapped.

He laughed.

"So *are* you going to hit me again?"

She let out an exasperated sigh. "No."

"Promise?"

"Pirate's honor," she said with aggravation.

"Then…" He leapt up, then reached down for her hand. She eyed his offering suspiciously, then accepted and let him help her to her feet. They were both still damp and sand-encrusted, but she was definitely different from the Captain Red Robert he had come to know. It was easy to see why she had come by the name. With the black wig gone, her own hair—even sea-tossed and salt-covered—was beautiful. It was a rich color, not as dark as Brendan's, but red and gold and still somehow deep and lustrous. Definitely unusual. He found himself imagining it clean and dry and cascading softly down her back in sunlight—or the moon's glow.

She cleared her throat.

"Water," she said. "We need to find water."

"Yes. Have you been shipwrecked before?" he asked.

"No. Have you?"

"No."

She smiled suddenly. "I *have* careened my ship in places similar to this, though."

"That's good. You won't be afraid."

"Afraid? Why would *I* be afraid?"

"Everyone is afraid of something."

"And what are you afraid of?" she asked him.

"Oh, I'm not so brave, really. I'm afraid of shot, swords, cannons…and of dying before making my mark on the world."

He had spoken lightly, but with the last words he had taken on an air of gravity. She studied him, frowning with concern.

"What?" he asked.

"I guess that's what I'm afraid of, too," she said.

"Cannon, shot and steel blades?" he queried.

"No. Well, I'd rather not be injured or lose a limb," she agreed. "But…it was the other. I just don't want to die before I've…"

"Really lived?"

"Well, that all depends on what you mean by 'living.'"

"Let's get on with this search for water, then we can discuss philosophy," he said. "Come on."

He led the way through the thick underbrush. If there were any trails through it, they were overgrown and long unused.

"What makes you think you can find water?" she called after him.

"Look around you."

"It does rain in the Caribbean," she reminded him.

"Do you have something better to do?"

"Maybe?"

"And that would be…?"

"We could build a fire on the beach, so my crew can find us," she said.

He was silent. Despite what he'd said earlier, there was no guarantee her crew had survived, and they both knew it.

"Okay, another ship," she said.

The idea made him uneasy. He wasn't sure why. Even if a merchantman were to find them, he wasn't a pirate, and with her red hair and bedraggled beauty, she would never be taken for the infamous Red Robert. Still, he was uneasy about the possibility of rescue.

Maybe it was because they were almost certainly in a pirate alley. Any ship that came upon them would probably be a pirate ship. And most pirate captains would either think his plight was amusing and leave him stranded or put him to work on their own ship. Or maybe just decide he should be slain on the spot.

The pirate code stated that no decent woman should be taken against her will. Female captives were usually ransomed. But the rules were not hard and fast. Red could be in serious trouble if they were discovered by the wrong ship.

And building a fire might bring the wrong kind of rescue.

And yet, what other option was there?

As they headed deeper into the brush, the going became harder. There were roots to trip over, and pebbles and rocks to cut their feet. The palm fronds grew low and thick. There were several varieties of palms, sea grape trees, fruit trees bearing what looked like little green limes and others apparently bearing figs, and more. The limes were a blessing, he thought. And there had to be a fresh water spring somewhere on the island.

"There!" he said suddenly, pointing.

He had broken through a grove of tall palms at the top of a small hill. And as he peered between the trunks, he could see a waterfall.

She crashed into his back, stumbling over one of the roots breaking through the thin layer of soil.

"It's…it's beautiful," she said.

Logan calculated they had come about half a mile from the beach. He didn't see any signs that the island was inhabited, but he had to wonder why. It offered the most important element of life—water. And there was enough real soil for vegetation to grow.

She pushed by him, eager to reach the water.

"Wait!"

She had fallen to her knees at the water's edge, but now she hesitated, water dripping from her cupped hands.

"Allow me," he said, walking up beside her. "The official taster, you know."

Despite his thirst, he only dabbed the water to his lips at first. It was sweet and clear. He sipped.

She was staring at him. He smiled. "Seems safe."

She drank. Then she sluiced water over her face, relishing the clean feel, before she drank again. He found himself watching her, relishing the delight she found in the fresh, cool sensation and the way she cast her head back to delight in the water pouring over her.

"It's a taste of heaven," she said.

Aye, a taste of heaven, he thought. Stranded he might be, but with clean, clear drinking water—and with her.

He rose and looked around.

"We should head back to the beach," he said.

"What? We just got here."

"And now that we've found water, we need to build a shelter."

She stared at him blankly for a moment, as if finally comprehending for the first time that they could be on this island for weeks, even months.

Or more.

Without a word, she turned around and started walking ahead of him toward the shore. He could hear her suck in her breath now and then, when she stepped on something hard or sharp.

Shoes would be nice, he thought. And a good strong knife or sword would be even better. He reached toward his calf, but in vain; he had lost his knife when he had cast off his boots.

Despite the pain to her delicate soles, she moved quickly. He kept close behind her.

She passed by a palm and held the branch out of her way; then it smacked him squarely in the face as he passed.

"Hey!" he yelled.

"Sorry," she said quickly.

But he could tell from her tone that she wasn't sorry at all. He wondered if she had let the branch snap back on purpose.

She reached the shore first and stood there, staring out at the waves. Just as there was often a calm before a storm, there was often one afterward, as well.

The world seemed to have been swept clean. The sea was like liquid glass, reflecting the glory of the sun. The sky was a soft blue, not a cloud to be seen. The roll of the surf against the sand was still like a sweet and pleasant whisper.

"I'll retrieve the barrel," he said. "The wood will be useful, and there might be something edible inside."

She followed more slowly as he strode down the beach toward the barrel that had saved their lives, then cried out suddenly, stumbling to her knees.

He turned back.

"What?" he asked in concern.

"Nothing!"

He walked back toward her anyway. She was sitting on the sand, holding her foot.

"Did you cut it?"

"I stepped on a shell."

"Let me see."

"No."

"Don't be such a…girl," he told her.

She cast him a dangerous glare, but she didn't say anything.

Hunkering down before her, he caught her wrist and moved her hand out of the way. Her foot was bleeding, but there was so much sand caked to her skin that he couldn't see how bad the gash might be.

"I'm all right," she said stiffly, pushing him away and starting to rise. Then she staggered slightly, and he rose quickly and lifted her into his arms, much to her indignation.

"Put me down!" she demanded.

He ignored her.

"Do what I tell you," she insisted. "I am the captain."

"You *were* a captain. So was I."

"I was captain last," she said irritably.

He ignored her, striding toward the water. She was an easy burden, despite the fact that she was stiff and totally uncooperative.

She slammed a fist against his chest.

"Hey! You promised not to hit me."

"I told you to put me down."

He had reached the water, and he was tempted.

"Damn you, Logan!"

He dropped her.

She went under, then came up quickly, sputtering and furious. She slapped at the hand he offered her. But when she staggered again, he caught hold of her anyway, to keep her from falling.

"We had to wash your foot," he explained.

Half standing, accepting his support to remain upright, she gave him her evil stare once again. "I'm soaked."

"You're the one who believes in bathing," he pointed out dryly.

"I thought you were concerned about my *foot?*"

"Actually, I am. An infection here could be serious. And saltwater will clean it and help heal it."

"So I needed an entire bath in saltwater…for my foot?"

He shrugged, picked her up again and headed the few feet to the beach. She swore, but he ignored her as he set her down easily and knelt at her side, taking her foot in his hand again. There was a slash right across her instep. He was grateful to notice that it didn't appear to be deep.

"Just a lot of blood, I think," he said lightly.

"It hurts," she admitted.

"Just sit here and let it soak in the waves for a few minutes," he told her as he ripped off a long strip of his bedraggled shirt. "Then we can wrap it up." His voice had grown husky. It was touching her that did it, he thought. Maybe he shouldn't have dropped her in the water. Her clothing was plastered to her body again, hugging her in a way that emphasized every perfect curve. The white cotton seemed to do more enhancing than concealing.

He stood quickly. He needed to get some distance from her.

"Where are you going?" she asked, frowning.

"Down the beach to get the barrel and do some exploring," he said lightly. "Who knows what treasures may lurk just around the bend? I'm sure we weren't the only ship caught up in that storm."

He left her, curious to see what might be in the barrel that had saved their lives.

Reaching it didn't help much. He had nothing with which to lever it open. The ship's cooper did an excellent job of sealing his creations, which helped preserve necessities on the ship. But now…

He managed to read the letters that had been burned into the side and realized that they had a barrel of rum—about a third full, judging by the weight, which had left enough room for the air that had made the barrel float and ensured their salvation.

Now he just needed tools to open it.

He looked back down the beach. Red was staring out at the sea. Her foot was in the water, though. The waves were inching up and crashing gently against the length of her slightly bent legs, and she'd folded her arms atop them. She looked like a mermaid cast up from the sea, not a far cry from the truth.

He stepped away from the annoying puzzle of the barrel and looked farther down the beach, where he saw numerous pieces of broken plank.

He hoped they weren't from the *Eagle,* and that Brendan, Peg-leg, Silent Sam, Hagar, Jimmy O'Hara and the rest were safe and figuring out how to rescue Red.

He started piling up the wood, mentally assembling the pieces into a shelter. His heart sank as he moved along; it was becoming obvious that at least one poor ship had broken up in the heavy winds and lashing waves of the storm.

He was definitely acquiring enough lumber.

After about a hundred yards, he came upon a large cargo chest. He stooped to examine it, then swore when he discovered that it was locked.

He found a thick rock and began slamming away at the padlock. When it was clear that he would never break the lock, he changed tactics and smashed in the lid of the chest, instead, then looked inside.

The chest had been well-built, with a strong seal that had kept out the ocean. The chest was filled with clothing, not the tools he would have preferred, and he saw breeches, bodices, skirts, dresses, silks, satins and lace. There were shoes and stockings, even jeweled brooches and collar pins.

He sat back on his heels, feeling relieved. He was certain that this haul had not come from their ship.

He was sorry, though, because he was certain an innocent merchantman had been destroyed in the storm, and the owners of the finery before him were now resting somewhere at the bottom of the sea, food for the fish.

He stood and looked out to sea. More and more

refuse was bobbing on the waves, washing up toward the shore. He ventured out to see what was coming his way.

Lots and lots of timbers, some with swatches of canvas sail and rigging caught around them. The rigging would be helpful in building, he thought.

And more barrels. He waded out deeper to retrieve the one floating closest. It had been staved in, he quickly realized, and was worthless.

He looked back toward Red again. She was up, a hand shielding her eyes from the sun as she, too, looked out to the deeper water. As he watched, she began to wade out, as he had been doing.

He didn't know what she had seen that had so drawn her attention. He started sloshing through the water to reach her position.

She stood stock-still. And then a cry escaped her, a cry so startled and shrill that his heart thundered.

"Red!"

He raced to reach her.

As he ran, he saw what had drawn her attention.

A man.

A man floating facedown in the water.

His sea-darkened hair was red, and he wore a coat similar to the one Brendan usually wore.

She was standing frozen in horror, so he stepped forward and, his heart in his throat, turned the body over.

CHAPTER SEVEN

THERE WAS A new ship in the harbor.

Using her spyglass, Sonya could see that it had taken some weather damage; men were even now busy repairing the mast.

There had been a storm; they'd seen it out at sea. But it hadn't taken a swipe at New Providence, and she was glad. It seemed to have taken a northeasterly path, perhaps cutting across Cuba and following the North American coast. She hoped it hadn't sunk Red Robert's *Eagle*.

All right, so she had taken some coins to betray Red Robert. This was a pirate island, after all, and in her own way, she was a pirate, too. It hadn't been personal. She had needed the money. And it had ended well, in any case.

But since the *Eagle* had sailed, she had been worried. She liked Red Robert, effeminate fop though he might be, but she had long had an ache in her heart for Haggerty. He lived within the law, but he seemed to understand those who were often forced to live on the other side of it. He was a man who abhorred violence, but he wasn't afraid of a fight. And when his eyes flashed with humor, she melted.

Even if he never wanted one of her girls. Or her.

She was jolted out of her thoughts when Blair Colm walked into the tavern.

It had been a slow morning. Though the storm had sent many a ship to this safe harbor for repair, the men had no time to go drinking. The able-bodied were busy at their work, sewing canvas, obeying the commands of the carpenters. The injured would be nursing their wounds, with the ships' physicians and even barbers sewing up flesh wounds and setting smashed limbs, or removing those that couldn't be saved.

Colm stared at her for a long while before speaking. He had been in before, and she took his money. After all, it spent just the same as anyone else's. But she had always hated the man, who was considered a monster by some and a hero by others.

She, for one, found it all too easy to believe the rumors that swirled about the man.

Rumors such as the one that said he had killed children by swinging them around by their heels and cracking their skulls open on rocks.

She felt a sudden wave of guilt. Red Robert might be effeminate, but the pirate had never been anything but decent to her. And she had betrayed him, knowing all the while that it was in the service of Blair Colm. True, the bald man had offered her a fine sum of money just to discover that Robert had left, and in what direction.

She had to survive, didn't she?

But she had known, deep down inside, that something evil was afoot, with a monster like Blair Colm seeking out Red Robert.

And she had taken the coins anyway.

"Sonya!"

She looked up.

"Captain Blair."

"Sir Captain Blair," he reminded her.

"Sir Captain Blair," she parroted.

"I'll have the private room, and your finest wench. No one old or worn out." He looked her up and down, to be sure she didn't miss the point that his insult had been directed specifically to her.

She only smiled and said, "As you wish."

"And your best rum. None of that rotgut you serve the drunkards."

"As you wish," she said again.

He still didn't move. She was dimly aware that the bar boys in the back had suddenly developed loose fingers and were dropping things. Blair Colm created such an atmosphere. He'd been known to backhand a lad or two for spilling a drop of rum.

"The room is yours, Sir Captain Blair," she said, hoping he would wait there for whatever poor girl she chose for him.

"You will join me."

She started. She was glad to be older and *worn out* when he was about.

"Aye?"

He let out something like a sniff. "I need information."

"I have no information."

"I believe you do."

He departed for the room. She rose slowly, afraid

not to follow. He'd not been kind to women who dissented, either.

She followed him in. "I can't see to your rum and services if I'm here," she said.

He took a seat against the wall. "Sit," he ordered her.

She sat with alacrity.

"Where did they go?" he demanded.

She stared at him, her mind genuinely blank. He was a big man. Muscular. But his features were sharp and vulpine. His hair and eyes were dark. He was English, but he had the look of a Spaniard. There was a sense of cruelty about the man, maybe in the very narrowness of his features, maybe in the way he moved, and maybe in those hellish dark eyes.

"They?"

"Red Robert and his crew."

"Oh. Yes, they were here, just before the storm," she said.

Blair Colm suddenly moved forward. It was the striking motion of a snake.

"Red Robert is coming after me, but that storm will hold him up."

"You tried to have him killed. Here," she said softly, guilt settling over her like a dark cloud.

He waved a hand dismissively. "I didn't try to have anyone killed. That wouldn't be honorable, now would it?" he asked quietly.

He was lying through his teeth, and they both knew it. She hated the man. All she wanted was to get away.

"They sailed out. They didn't say where they were heading."

Before she knew it, he was on his feet, holding her by the hair in front of him. "Red Robert took a ship before he got here and is traveling with a captive."

"Yes!" she cried out. He had her dead against him. She could feel strands of hair tearing from her scalp. Her heart was thundering.

She could scream, but she knew no one would come.

"The captive is Lord Haggerty," he said.

"Yes," she said again, and this time the word was a whimper. She had always thought herself hardened, inside and out. She had seen so much. She had slept with more men than most women ever knew. She despised them, as they despised her.

But now she was afraid.

He stared at her hard. "They are coming after me. Together. They are hunting me."

"I know nothing of that!" she insisted, frantic. "Think! Would they discuss their business with the likes of me?"

He leaned closer, eyes peering into hers. "Many men speak to you, wench."

What the hell did he want her to say?

"Perhaps they *are* seeking you out. I don't know. They sailed into the storm—they're probably all dead. Let me go!"

"Not yet. Now, the real question. *Who* is Red Robert?"

"What?"

Another jerk on her hair. Pain shot through her skull. Tears pooled in her eyes.

"Red Robert is…Red Robert," she said, tears of fear and pain springing to her eyes.

"Liar!"

She found herself flung onto the table. He was quickly on top of her. "The truth! I'll have the truth."

"I don't know! I swear to God, I don't know!" He was straddling her, and she knew fighting back was foolish, but she couldn't help herself.

She spat at him.

She should have expected it. He slapped her with a vengeance that knocked her unconscious, though for far too short a time.

She vaguely felt him rise, felt him shuffle her skirt out of his way. Too weak to fight, too groggy even to protest, she simply turned away. She never said a word.

And when he was done, he dropped a coin on the table as he casually straightened his breeches. "Who does know?"

"Bend down, kiss your arse and die," she managed to respond.

She was ready for the next blow. It was worth it.

"I'll find Teach and ask *him*," he said.

She laughed, not bothering to rise. "By all means, find him," she suggested. "He'll help you bend over, kiss your arse and die."

One last blow and he was gone.

Not even then did she burst into tears.

She told herself that she was too hard, but in reality she was simply too numb.

When she finally rose, she went to talk with her girls, and she told them that he had the littlest penis she'd ever seen and couldn't keep hard long enough to finish.

The girls would talk. It would be all over the island.

She began praying that Red Robert *would* find him on the high seas.

And that Robert did indeed intend to kill him.

LOGAN HESITATED, but they had to know the truth, one way or the other.

The dead man was floating facedown.

Red stared at the corpse, stricken, as he had never imagined she might be. Brave pirate, brave *actress*. She loved her cousin. She looked unbelievably fragile and vulnerable now, and he was afraid himself. He didn't want to turn the body over, because he felt helpless in the face of her obvious distress.

He swallowed hard. One lesson life had taught him: face all demons. Nothing could change what was, and acceptance allowed you to move on.

He turned the body over.

She gasped, and stepped back shaking.

It wasn't Brendan but some other poor soul. The fish had already been nibbling at his nose, and he was a pathetic and dreadful sight.

But he wasn't Brendan.

Logan reached out to Red to steady her. And for a moment, she leaned on his strength. Then she pulled away, as if furious with him. But she wasn't angry with him, and he knew it. She was angry with herself. Red Robert, who had mastered her act so long ago, was ruing her own show of weakness.

But the sight of the corpse was a horrible one. The

corpse had bloated in the water, and now he had the macabre appearance of something unreal, something that had never been human.

"I'll bury him," he said curtly.

"He—he isn't one of ours," she whispered.

"Whoever he is, he deserves a decent burial." He didn't add that a rotting corpse on the beach would create a horrible miasma. He turned, pulling the corpse through the shallows as he paralleled the beach. She was still for a moment; then he heard a splashing behind him as she followed to help.

He dragged the body up to a cluster of palm trees far above the water.

He didn't want high tide undoing his work.

He still hadn't found any tools, but a broken coconut made a crude scoop. Fifteen minutes later, when he was already dripping with sweat from the effort of working with so small a tool, he looked over and saw that she had gone back down the beach to discover a large silver soup tureen, which made a much better scoop, and had started digging alongside him.

"Let me," he said.

She was working vigorously and didn't even look up at him. She shook her head, intent on her task. She worked almost as if she were in a frenzy, burning her strength. He let her, certain she was trying to allay her fear that although the body they had found was not Brendan, the crew of her ship might have met a similar fate. When he was certain she had burned away most of her emotion, he stepped forward again, reaching for the silver tureen, forcing her to look at him. "You've done more in a matter of minutes than I did in twenty. Let me finish," he said gently.

She stared at him, blinked, lowered her head and nodded at last.

The tureen was a big help. His shoulders and back ached, but in the end, he managed a deep-enough grave. He pulled the man in and was ready to drop the sand back over him when she stopped him.

"Wait."

"Yes?" he said, and eyed her expectantly.

"Don't you…know a few words to say?"

"Don't you?"

"You're a captain."

"So are you."

"I've never lost a crew member," she said proudly.

"Neither have I," he informed her.

"But you—"

"I what?"

"You still believe in God," she said flatly.

He looked at her for a moment. *So do you,* he wanted to tell her, but something in her eyes told him to keep the words inside.

"Father, accept the soul of this, thy servant," he said instead, and crossed himself.

"And may ye be in heaven an hour before the devil knows ye're dead!" she said, and did likewise.

Strange prayer for a man who was already dead.

"Amen," he said, and she turned away.

Scooping the sand back on wasn't half as hard as digging it out. He was done in a matter of minutes. To his surprise, she had fashioned a cross out of palm fronds, and when he had finished, she set it into the sand covering the body.

"It won't stay, you know," he said gently.

"Ah, but it's there for the journey," she replied.

She turned away and started walking back down the beach. As she left, he felt his stomach rumble. Without the labor to take his mind off things, his body was reminding him that they hadn't eaten.

Well, if nothing else, there were coconuts. And rum.

But hunger didn't seem to be plaguing Red yet, as she examined the flotsam that continued to wash up on the beach. He followed her, collecting timber, then shouted out with triumph, seeing what appeared to be a chest of carpenter's tools next to a broken crate.

"Aha!"

"What?" she cried, startled and clearly afraid of what he might have found.

He was already down on his knees beside the chest, pounding at the lock with a sharp stone. When it split apart in his hand, he didn't care, he just picked up another one and resumed his efforts.

Finally the ring holding the lock in place gave, and he looked up at her, smiling in triumph, feeling as if he had just stumbled on a cache of gold doubloons.

"Nails! We have nails. And a hammer, a lathe…and a leather needle…!"

She didn't respond with the same enthusiasm.

"What?" he asked her.

"It's not…ours, is it?" she whispered.

He sat back on his haunches. "There are no markings," he told her.

She let out a sigh. "Ours had initials. It isn't ours."

"There's been nothing on this beach to suggest that the *Eagle* broke up," he assured her.

She looked reassured, at least for the moment.

"All right, take the chest," he said.

"Me?"

"Unless you want to carry the lumber?"

"And where are we going?" she demanded.

He rose and looked around, then pointed out a place a good twenty yards farther inland and a good hundred yards to the east of their hasty cemetery. Palm trees surrounded a glade where their shade had kept the earth barren of brush and scrub.

"Come on, let's go," he said.

"I'm the captain here," she insisted.

"Fine. You build the shelter."

"I am willing for you to be the carpenter."

"Ah. And were you going to sit somewhere on your arse while I worked?" he demanded. "That's no captain's privilege, not on a pirate ship."

"No, I was simply...setting the record straight."

"Let's move."

"You are still my prisoner."

"Indeed? Well, I'm a hungry prisoner who knows that night will come. And that it may rain again. And I'd like to get a shelter rigged up. So I hope you'll excuse me if I don't pretend I'm in chains and you're wearing a brace of pistols."

She picked up the chest of tools and started ahead of him, then stepped back and watched while he plotted the strength of the trees and their position. He quickly set forth flattening his chosen ground and mentally drawing the dimensions of the abode he intended to erect, and then got started with timber and nails, creating a frame. He couldn't have been happier with his find.

He realized she was missing at one point and began cursing beneath his breath. Had she gone from being a pirate to a princess?

But as he turned to head back to the beach to look for her, he heard the sound of something being dragged along the sand.

She was bringing back a huge mass of canvas.

A sail from the broken ship that had given them both the cargo and the corpse.

Tugging the canvas, she looked slim and frail. And yet he realized that though she *was* slim, she was well-muscled, and that all her pretending and parading as a pirate had certainly given her an excellent physique. But she was tiring, so he hurried forward to help.

"I thought we might be in need of a roof," she said dryly.

"I had certainly planned on one," he said. "But palm fronds would have sufficed."

"Canvas will be better."

"I agree."

She actually smiled.

"So you admit I've been helpful," she said.

The canvas was heavy. He had to admit it: he was impressed that she had lugged it so far. "I'm going to take part of it up that tree to get leverage, then drag it over the frame. I'll need your help, handing it up to me."

"Aye, aye," she said, but she looked irritated.

"What?"

She didn't say anything, just pushed the canvas toward him. With the first side done, he had to climb down, then shimmy up a farther tree, so he could lean out across the frame and pull the canvas over and down. He just managed not to let her see that he nearly fell during the effort. The near miss sobered him. It was one thing to be stranded on the island. It would be quite another to be stranded there with a broken leg.

When he came down from the second tree, he was sweating and exhausted. Red must have been tired, as well, but she didn't complain, and she looked at their pathetic little structure without criticism.

"Well?" he said.

"Bugs," she said.

"Bugs?"

"Bugs come out at night."

"The mosquitoes will no doubt make a meal of us—unless the poor souls on that ship carried netting."

"What about food?"

"We can start here," he told her, catching hold of a coconut, a chisel and a hammer. He could break a coconut with the best of them. He offered her a half, sloshing with coconut milk.

"Drink up."

Thirst won out over manners. She slurped at the milk and started to gnaw at the meat. He tossed her a knife from the chest. She caught it deftly and dug into the meat. He turned his attention to his own half, realizing he was ravenous.

"Back down the beach?" she asked, when they were done with their impromptu meal.

"Back down the beach," he agreed.

He brought the hammer and chisel. This time, he made quick work of the barrels.

They had a lot of rum.

And rancid water.

But finally the fifth barrel yielded dried biscuit.

They both dug in. It didn't have any taste whatsoever, but at least it was free of weevils, and Logan knew that it would, at least, sustain them. But after a few bites, Red was on her feet again.

"Done already?"

She graced him with a smile. They were both sweaty and dirty, but there was something appealing about the streaks on her face.

"I haven't begun, but we need to build a fire."

He looked out at the sea. They needed to be rescued, but he was still afraid of the wrong ship coming upon them.

He stood, still chewing. The biscuit was…hard.

"All right," he said, after he managed to swallow. "You want to boil water and soften this?"

She flashed him another surprise smile. "And improve it," she assured him.

She grabbed the tools and started searching through the rest of the barrels. She seemed to be looking for something specific, and when she found it, she cried out with pleasure as she opened it. "Logan! We've got sugar!" she cried happily. "And it's well bagged in burlap and…where's the fire?" she inquired sweetly.

He turned with a rueful shrug and started searching for something with which to spark a flame.

"No flint?" she asked him hopefully.

He glared at her. "My pockets, madam, are empty."

As he began hiking wearily toward the trees in search of rocks and twigs for fire-starting, he heard her cry out with pleasure once again.

"What, you've found a lit candle?" he called to her.

But she hadn't found a candle. Instead—and even better—she had found a magnifying glass. She raced toward the trees, seeking the driest tinder she could find. Dead fronds would easily catch fire.

But they would need branches to keep it going.

There were plenty of the latter near their hut, and he went that way. A minute later, she brought her collection of dry vegetation to the spot where he was arranging their firewood. The sun was already beginning to set, he realized, and he longed to take the glass from her hand to speed the task, but she was determined. At last the tinder lit. He blew on it gently, and the flame grew. In moments the branches were burning and they had a real fire, although a rather smokey one, since apparently not all the wood was as dry as it had appeared.

"It's a dreadful fire," she said.

"It's a fire."

She rose. "Where is that soup tureen?" She went for it, then ran back for the sugar and biscuit. "Water!" she called to him. "We need fresh water."

He muttered beneath his breath and followed her. Rummaging again, he found a pitcher and a silver teapot, and went off to fill them both. When he returned, he found that she had come up with a skillet and was already carefully warming it at the fire. She took the teapot from him and poured a small amount into the pan, then added the biscuit and sugar.

Then she looked at the pitcher.

He handed it to her. "Drink slowly."

She didn't. She finished every drop. Then she looked at him guiltily.

"It's all right. I did the same thing at the spring."

She flushed.

"I'll go see if we have plates," he offered.

They did. He was frankly surprised more bodies hadn't washed up on the shore, given how much cargo had appeared. One trunk contained service for twenty in fine Chinese porcelain. There was silver, as well. He decided to drag the whole trunk back to their shelter, on the theory that it was better to have more than they needed than nothing at all.

He brought over silverware and two plates, and sat cross-legged before the fire. He started to fork out a piece of the biscuit turned to sugar cakes, but she spoke while he was in midmotion.

"Actually, it would be good to have a grog now," she said, looking at him.

He looked back at her, ready to remind her that she was constantly striving to prove her self-sufficiency, but instead he rose and headed down the beach. He dragged back the sugar barrel first, then went back for the partially filled barrel of rum that had brought them to the island. When he returned, he saw that she had gotten up, as well, and came back dragging another of the trunks.

"Teacups," she told him.

"Ah."

Then, smiling, she mixed them each a grog of sugar, water and rum.

At last they were seated at the fire again. The biscuit was far better now that it had been soaked with sugar, and he had to admit the grog was smooth, seeming to heat and ease his muscles all at once. They ate in silence, still ravenous, and he knew they made a ridiculous picture, seated with their fine china before a crude fire and their palm tree, broken lumber and canvas shelter.

Maybe it was exhaustion.

Maybe it was the rum.

Maybe it was the setting sun painting the sky with streaks of orange and pink. The colored sky kissed the water, and the waves washed with a gentle and soothing rhythm onto the beach.

Whatever the cause, it was an oddly peaceful moment.

He realized his shirt was torn and ragged, his breeches frayed, and they were both streaked with dirt. Red's hair was wild and as wickedly colored as the sunset. Her clothing, as tattered as his own, still seemed to hug her body. And she had never appeared more alluring to him.

He finished his grog, made himself another.

She arched a brow but said nothing.

"What, Captain?" he muttered, fighting to keep his distance from her. "You had wanted me to take the helm?"

"We're not done," she told him.

"Oh?"

"We need blankets."

"I could sleep here and now."

"But…you won't."

He grinned slowly, relaxing after the hard work of the day. "Blankets. Should I find a mattress, as well?"

"You are not amusing, you know."

"Ah, but you…it's so hard to decide just what you are—Captain Robert."

"There is nothing to decide. I am exactly what you see."

"Really? That from someone who dresses up like a man and pretends to be the terror of the sea?"

"I *am* the terror of the sea," she informed him coldly.

"And after just one man."

She stared at him. "You are more complex."

"Me? I am an open book."

"Ah, yes. *Laird* Haggerty. Maybe now. But I sense it was not always so."

"No," he admitted. "I came from war, treachery, murder, betrayal…"

"And ended up with a good life."

"I was taken in by a good man."

"Taken in?" she asked softly.

"I served him, and served him well. But he was a kind man, and had no son of his own, and I grew to love him like a son. And then came the Act of Union, and I was a laird again. A letter from the old country made it so."

"You are a lucky man."

"I let myself be lucky."

She started to laugh. "You think a person chooses to have good luck or bad?"

"I think a person can choose to let the past take control and simmer until there is nothing left in their heart except hatred."

"Hatred can keep a person alive," she said.

"And hatred can consume a person from within," he warned.

"And you hate no one?"

"Aye, Captain. I know how to hate. But I wanted to find life, as well."

She shook her head, looking away. "You fell in love," she told him.

He hesitated. "I fell into good company," he said.

"What about your dear Cassandra?"

"She is…proper."

"She must love you very much."

"She is a loving person."

She rose. "Well, fear not, Laird Haggerty. There's every hope that we shall get off this island, and, as I told you, there is no need for ransom. You are a free man."

She spoke strangely. He didn't remind her that he was a free man already. They were both free.

And they were both prisoners. Of an island.

She walked off down the beach. He rose and joined her. As the sun set, it was growing cool, and he saw that she was shivering.

He strode past her, searching again. There were broken barrels littering the beach, those they had split, and still more to be opened. The refuse covered half a mile, he thought. There was a great deal still to be explored and discovered.